From "Shortcut" by Nancy Werlin

As if it were yesterday rather than more than four years ago, Lacey could see Rhonda tossing Catrine's cupcake box on the sidewalk. Laughing. "Come on, Lacey, smash it!" she'd said, and jumped forward. And then Lacey could see her own small yellow-sneakered foot rising into the air. And then stomping downward on top of Catrine's chocolate birthday cupcakes. Left, left. Right, right.

Here, now, in science lab, Lacey felt her legs tremble. Involuntarily, she glanced down at her feet.

Okay. Fine. Fine, then.

When the bell rang, Lacey would run. She would intercept Catrine before Catrine started to take the shortcut home. She would warn her.

This once.

Lacey watched the clock. She swallowed the lump in her throat. Fifteen seconds. Fourteen. Thirteen . . .

✦ ✦ ✦

Readers "will find plenty of stereotypic geeks and nerds, but they'll also find outsiders who are unexpected . . . [and] may make them think about who's 'in' and who's 'out' and why." —*Booklist*

OTHER SPEAK BOOKS

On the Fringe

On the Fringe

Edited by
Donald R. Gallo

speak
An Imprint of Penguin Putnam Inc.

SPEAK
Published by the Penguin Group
Penguin Putnam Books for Young Readers,
345 Hudson Street, New York, New York 10014, U.S.A.
Penguin Books Ltd, 80 Strand, London WC2R 0RL, England
Penguin Books Canada Ltd, 10 Alcorn Avenue, Toronto, Ontario, Canada M4V 3B2

Penguin Books Ltd, Registered Offices: Harmondsworth, Middlesex, England

First published in the United States of America by Dial Books,
a division of Penguin Putnam Inc., 2001
Published by Speak, an imprint of Penguin Putnam Inc., 2003

3 5 7 9 10 8 6 4 2

Copyright © Donald R. Gallo, 2001
"Geeks Bearing Gifts" copyright © Ron Koertge, 2001
"Great Expectations" copyright © M. E. Kerr, 2001
"Shortcut" copyright © Nancy Werlin, 2001
"Through a Window" copyright © Angela Johnson, 2001
"Muzak for Prozac" copyright © Jack Gantos, 2001
"Standing on the Roof Naked" copyright © Francess Lantz, 2001
"Mrs. Noonan" copyright © Graham Salisbury, 2001
"WWJD" copyright © Will Weaver, 2001
"Satyagraha" copyright © Alden R. Carter, 2001
"A Letter from the Fringe" copyright © Joan Bauer, 2001
"Guns for Geeks" copyright © Chris Crutcher, 2001

Teen quotes in this book's introduction taken from "Voices From The
Hellmouth" by Jon Katz on *www.slashdot.org*.
Reprinted with permission of the author.

All rights reserved
Text set in Meridien

THE LIBRARY OF CONGRESS HAS CATALOGED THE DIAL EDITION AS FOLLOWS:
On the fringe / edited by Donald R. Gallo.
p. cm.
Contents: Geeks bearing gifts /Ron Koertge—Great expectations / M. E. Kerr
Shortcut / Nancy Werlin—Through a window / Angela Johnson—Muzak for
Prozac / Jack Gantos—Standing on the roof naked / Francess Lantz—Mrs.
Noonan / Graham Salisbury—WWJD / Will Weaver—Satyagraha /Alden R.
Carter—A letter from the fringe / Joan Bauer—Guns for geeks / Chris Crutcher.
ISBN 0-8037-2656-2
I. High schools—Juvenile fiction. 2. Children's stories, American.
[I. High schools—Fiction. 2. Schools—Fiction. 3. Short stories.]
I. Gallo, Donald R.
PZ5.O9355 2001
[Fic]—dc21 00-040521

Speak ISBN 0-14-250026-7

Printed in the United States of America

This book is dedicated
to every kid who has
ever been called
a hurtful name.

And to every kid who
has tried to feel superior
by putting down
someone else.

Contents

Acknowledgments

THIS BOOK EXISTS only because writers Fran Lantz, Jackie French Koller, and Sandy Salisbury almost simultaneously said, Why don't you do a collection of stories about . . . ? Recognizing the good sense in their recommendations, I began to explore the possibilities with various other authors and the concept took shape.

And then on one of the Internet listservs about books for young people that I subscribe to, author Nancy Werlin distributed page after page of comments from disenfranchised teenagers describing the harassment they endure from their schoolmates because they are different, and expressing their frustration with school administrators who in the aftermath of the Columbine shootings were making their lives even harder.

It is to these four professional writers and those teenagers that I owe my greatest thanks.

A big thank-you (and a hug) goes to my wife, C. J. Bott, for her thoughtful ideas and supportive suggestions whenever I sought her advice.

Thanks also to Lauri Hornik and the people at Dial Books for recognizing the need for these kinds of stories.

ACKNOWLEDGMENTS

Introduction

IF YOU'VE EVER been to a chicken farm or seen a photograph of the inside of a commercial henhouse, you may have noticed that all the chickens look alike. It's not just because they are bred that way. They themselves insist on it. If a chicken looks different in any way from the rest—if it is weak, injured, or deformed—the others will begin to pick on it. Literally. They will peck it to death.

We humans may not be as nasty as chickens, but you know that there is a pecking order among students in your school, at every grade. The biggest and strongest continually pick on classmates who look odd, dress differently, are overweight or small and scrawny, come from a different part of town, have unusual interests, or have a different sexual orientation. If you are a nonconforming student, at best you're excluded; most often you're verbally harassed and sometimes physically assaulted. Some of the students who put others down and treat classmates cruelly are those most often admired by teachers and honored by administrators: the athletes and student government leaders.

Most of the time, the oddballs in your school survive on internal strength alone, lying low, staying out of the way. A few others may flaunt their differentness by dyeing their hair garish pink or blue and goofing loudly in the hallways. A few students have even hurt so much and felt so alone that they've killed themselves. Once in a while one of those students will strike back, as Eric Harris and Dylan Klebold did at Columbine High School in Littleton, Colorado, on April 20, 1999. Unable to take the abuse any longer, they lashed out in the most harmful way possible, killing twelve students and one teacher, physically wounding several other people, and emotionally scarring the entire community.

Since that horrible day, school faculties, administrators, student groups, community leaders, politicians, and the media have all given more attention to the problems of school violence, access to guns, and violence in games on the Internet. As they should. But few people have looked beyond the physical evidence at the emotional and social conditions that brought on that violence. Few people have looked at the feelings of alienation, frustration, hurt, and anger felt by teenage students whom the rest of the school community calls *weirdos, geeks, nerds, freaks, faggots,* and worse.

In fact, since Columbine, life for oddball students in middle schools and high schools across the nation has become worse, not better. Shortly after the Columbine shooting, alienated kids filled chat rooms and message boards on the Internet with tales of mistreatment and cries for recognition and understanding. Perhaps you've had experiences similar to these.

A teenager in New Jersey explained how he feels every day:

> Day by day, it's like they take pieces out of you,
> like a torture, one at a time. My school has 1,500

kids. I could never make a sports team. I have never been to a party. I sit with my friends at our own corner of the cafeteria. If we tried to join the other kids, they'd throw up or leave. And by now, I'd rather die. Sometimes, I do feel a lot of real pure rage. And I feel better when I go online. Sometimes I think the games keep me from shooting anybody, not the other way around. 'Cause I can get even there, and I'm pretty powerful there. But I'd never do it. Something much deeper was wrong with these kids in Colorado.

A student from Idaho explained how he was treated by his school's administration:

I wrote an article for my school paper. The advisor suggested we write about "our feelings" about Colorado. My feelings—what I wrote—were that society is blaming the wrong things. You can't blame screwed-up kids or the Net. These people don't know what they were talking about. How 'bout blaming a system that takes smart or weird kids and drives them crazy? How about understanding why these kids did what they did, 'cause in some crazy way, I feel something for them. For their victims, too, but for them. I thought it was a different point-of-view, but important. I was making a point. I mean, I'm not going to the prom. You know what? The article was killed, and I got sent home with a letter to my parents. It wasn't an official suspension, but I can't go back until Tuesday. And it was made pretty clear to me that if I made any noise about it, it would be a suspension or worse. So this is how they are trying to figure out what happened in Colorado, I guess. By blaming a sub-culture . . . They pretend to want to have a "dialogue" but . . . what they really want to know is who's dangerous to them.

Another teen described a similar experience:

I stood up in a social studies class—the teacher wanted a discussion—and said I could never kill anyone or condone anyone who did kill anyone. But that I could, on some level, understand these kids in Colorado, the killers. Because day after day, slight after slight, exclusion after exclusion, you can learn how to hate, and that hatred grows and takes you over sometimes, especially when you come to see that you're hated only because you're smart and different, or sometimes even because you are online a lot, which is still so uncool to many kids. After the class, I was called to the principal's office and told that I had to agree to undergo five sessions of counseling or be expelled from school, as I had expressed "sympathy" with the killers in Colorado, and the school had to be able to explain itself if I "acted out." In other words, for speaking freely, and to cover their ass, I was not only branded a weird geek, but a potential killer.

* * *

Months after the shooting rampage, some student leaders at Columbine High School refused to see how their behavior was wrong in any way. In an interview with a *Time* magazine reporter, a member of the football team said:

> "Columbine is a clean, good place except for those rejects [referring to Harris, Klebold, and kids like them] . . . Sure, we teased them. But what do you expect with kids who come to school with weird hairdos and horns on their hats? It's not just jocks; the whole school's disgusted with them. They're a bunch of homos. . . . If you want to get rid of someone, usually you tease 'em. So the whole school would call them homos. . . ." (December 20, 1999)

With those kinds of attitudes and issues in mind, we started this book, inviting a number of highly respected authors to write short stories about teenagers who don't fit into the mainstream in a variety of ways: kids who can't afford to dress in brand-name clothes, who are unathletic or overweight, who live on the wrong side of the tracks, who wear unusual makeup and body decorations, who are not heterosexual, who are members of a racial minority, who have different belief systems. The stories examine conformity, popularity, peer pressure, and harassment among teenagers like yourself, in schools similar to yours.

These stories, published here for the first time, don't attempt to solve the problems in your school or to place blame (though athletes get hit pretty hard in this collection). These stories are here, first of all, to engage you. But we also hope they provide glimpses into the minds of teenagers who are different from their more popular peers and will offer you thought-provoking experiences that may result in greater understanding and tolerance of others.

On the Fringe

Geeks Bearing Gifts

Ron Koertge

When Renee sets out to interview the nonconformists and outcasts at Roosevelt High for a newspaper article, she has no idea what to expect. "I just want to talk to people who are different, that's all," she tells one group. William asks, "Different from you?" "I mean different from everybody," she says. Boy, does she have a lot to learn.

"HEY, RENEE. WASSUP?"

"Hi, Willard. Nothing special. How about you? Ready to play Central this Friday?"

"Yeah, I guess." He winced and reached across to massage his left shoulder. "Listen, Bobby tells me you writin' about people who're left out of things, is that right?"

"Sort of, yeah. There's this journalism scholarship I'm eligible for, and I need one more strong piece. So I thought of doing something in-depth about outsiders."

"And you weren't gonna talk to me?"

"Willard, are you kidding? You're on the football team; you're the Walter Payton of Roosevelt High."

"So?"

"So you walk down the halls, everybody says hi."

"So?"

"So you can't be an outsider if everybody wants to be your friend."

"Sayin' hi don't mean they my friends."

"Well, they look up to you, then."

He shook his head so hard that the beads woven into his dreadlocks clicked together. "First semester, maybe. Football season over, and I'm like nobody."

"No way. You're still the man."

"Renee, when I'm playin' ball, they happy to know me. That be over, they just wary of me."

"No way."

"Don't you watch TV? I'm a big black guy. All we do is drink malt liquor and jack cars."

Renee frowned. "Don't talk that way."

"Listen here, girl. I'm a black man in a white world. Only difference between me and some brother lyin' dead in the street is I can catch a football."

"So you're inside when you're playing ball but outside when you're not."

"Playin' ball I don't think about it. So it's like a little reprieve."

Renee put her books down with a thud. "I'm not so sure this is going to work."

Her boyfriend, Bobby, lowered the burrito he was gnawing on. "Why not, baby?"

"I was talking to Willard and—"

"Did he come on to you?"

"What? No. He was just, I don't know, different."

"Different how?"

"Different from what I imagined, I guess. Did he ever say anything to you about how playing football is like a reprieve?"

"A what?"

"Do you ever talk to Willard?"

"Only every day."

"No, no. That's just, 'Did you catch ESPN last night?' I mean really talk to him."

When Bobby frowned, his eyebrows almost met. "About what?"

"He just got me thinking, that's all." She looked right at her boyfriend, right at the blue eyes beneath the cropped bleached hair. "Do you think black people are left out of a lot of things?"

"Baby, Tiger Woods is only like a gazillionaire."

"I mean regular black people."

"Honey, regular *white* people are left out of things."

Renee stood up. "I don't know anything about being an outsider. I'm gonna find something else to write about."

Bobby shrugged. "If this was football, Coach would call you a quitter."

"Well, it's not football, it's journalism."

"Show some guts anyway. No pain, no gain."

Renee stopped beside the crowded table in the northwest corner of the cafeteria.

"Can I talk to you guys a minute?" she asked.

Marco pulled his tray closer, then leaned protectively over a giant Pepsi, two Twinkies, and some Little Debbie snacks. "What about?"

"I'm doing this piece for the school newspaper. It's about outsiders, rebels, that kind of thing."

"Oh," said Lawrence. "That's us all right. Except instead of motorcycles we take the bus. Our tattoos say BORN TO TRANSFER."

"Just get out of here," ordered Marco.

"Look, I just want to get you guys' side of—"

Marco stood up. "Didn't you hear me? Are you death?"

Renee frowned.

"He means deaf. He's got auditory dyslexia." William didn't even look up from the book he was reading.

Renee tugged at the cover until William lowered it slowly, like a drawbridge that would let everyone into the walled city. "I just want to talk to people who are different, that's all."

"Different from you?" asked William as everyone at the table nodded.

"No. I mean yes. I mean different from everybody."

William glanced at his friends. "That narrows it right down."

Renee pushed her blond hair back. "Okay, wait. Make it people out of the mainstream, then."

"Nonconformists."

"Sort of."

"Outcasts."

"Kind of."

"The generally quaint."

"No."

"Bohemian?"

"Not exactly. Where did you learn all those words, anyway? I thought you guys were—"

"Retarded."

"No."

"Yeah, right."

Renee dropped her books, exasperated. "All right. Yes. Satisfied?"

William grinned. "Ah, the truth—it rings like a bell, doesn't it?"

"So tell the truth, then." She turned to Marco. "What's it like to have auditory dyslexia?"

"It sucks, big time."

Renee took a notebook out of her backpack. "Okay, that's good. Tell me more."

Marco took a bite of Twinkie and sputtered. "I don't want to tell you more. Just get out of here, you nosy beach!"

Renee frowned and looked at William.

"Do I really have to translate that for you?" he asked.

Lawrence stood up. "Wait, you guys. Don't be so rude." He dug into his scratched briefcase, flipping the duct-taped handle out of the way. "Take this," he said, handing her a matchbox.

"What is it?"

"Just a little something," Lawrence said, "to make up for Marco's attitude."

She looked at it warily. "This is a trick, isn't it?"

"Open it."

"Tell me what it is first."

"Toenails."

Renee screamed and the matchbox went flying.

"Beware," Lawrence crowed, "of geeks bearing gifts!"

Still laughing, Marco and Lawrence picked up their things and staggered away.

Renee sat down next to William. "My God."

"That was pretty clever, actually," said William. "A nice pun, and well executed."

Renee shook her head. "How come they won't talk to me?"

"To start with, this is probably the first time in, like, three and a half years you even looked this way. Are they gonna believe all of a sudden you're totally interested in them?"

"But I'm a journalist."

"Renee, you're a cheerleader." He stood up. "Anybody want anything? I'm going to get some dessert."

Renee turned to Monique. "Will you talk to me?"

"Sure. I'll tell you my life story: My parents took one look at me, then left me on a mountainside to die. A pack of dogs found me and brought me up, which is fine until a cat walks by. Then I kind of lose it."

"Can you just tell me what it's like to be, uh, you know, visually challenged?"

"You mean blind as a bat?"

"Okay, fine—what's it like to be blind as a bat?"

"Well, it really sucks." She looked down. "Like, right now I can't hardly see my stupid pudding, okay? And if I want to read something, I have to hold it about two inches away from my face like some total freak. *And* it's just gonna get worse and worse until I go like totally blind. Then I get a white cane, which is every girl's ideal fashion accessory."

"When will you not be able to see at all?"

Monique shook her head. "I don't know."

"And there's nothing anybody can do?"

"Probably not. Pretty soon I'll be applying to Guide

Dogs for the Blind, get screened, take the training, and score this cool pooch I get along with. Then we'll kick back and listen to dirty books on tape."

"You're kidding."

"Hey, Miss Perfect Pants. Just because we're disabled doesn't mean we're dead."

"Wow." Renee patted her notebook. "Can I use that?" She started writing.

"Listen." Monique scooted her chair closer to Renee. "William calls us 'The Unwelcome.' But he says we perform this service to mankind."

Renee looked up. "Like what?"

"Well, you're at one end of the scale, okay? People think, 'If only I was as cute as Renee or as popular as Renee' or whatever. But we're at the other end: 'At least I can see better than Monique.' Or 'At least I don't drool like Marco.'"

"People really think stuff like that?"

"You don't?"

William put a paper plate in front of the girls. "I got everybody something anyway."

Monique held out her hand. "Renee, spell out brownie on my palm and we'll do a scene from *The Miracle Worker*." Then she stood up. "I'll catch you guys later."

"Is she always that way?" Renee asked.

"What way?"

"You know, kind of bitter and thorny."

"She doesn't want to be pathetic." When Renee reached for her pen, he added, "Don't write that down." William turned his brownie one way, then another. "I thought of something," he said finally, "as I was standing in line. A guy named Colin Wilson wrote a book called *The Outsider*. You should read it for your article."

"For sure." Renee twisted her gold Cross pen. "What's it about?"

He rolled his eyes up. "Let me see if I can get this straight. An outsider is somebody engaged in an intense self-exploration, somebody who's willing to challenge cultural values. Something like that."

"That's cool."

"Exactly. But that's not us. Colin Wilson meant Kakfa and Camus and van Gogh. Monique and Lawrence and Marco and I, we're just barely holding on most of the time."

"But I could write about that. Everybody knows you guys are in the Resource Room, but half the kids in school think it's a good deal 'cause you get all that extra help."

William took two prescription bottles out of his pocket. "I'm like this guitar that has to constantly be tuning itself. Otherwise, my strings snap!"

"Really? Every day?"

"Pretty much."

Renee's beeper started to chirp but she turned it off. "Tell me about that, okay?"

Renee scowled at her keyboard when the phone rang. But it didn't stop, so finally she hit Save and picked up the receiver.

"Man, are you hard to get hold of," said Bobby. "Where've you been?"

"Interviewing people. I decided not to give up on this piece."

"I saw you talking to that stoner William."

"Except that he's not. Those pills are totally necessary, from a doctor and everything. And he has to sort of pay attention to himself all day so he doesn't get too, you know, too much Wellbutrin or not enough Ritalin. He was pretty interesting."

"Did he come on to you?"

"God, Bobby. Not everybody comes on to me, okay?"

"Well, they should. You're really pretty. Especially with your clothes off."

"Will you shut up! My mom's home."

"This is your private line, dummy. Nobody's gonna—"

"And don't call me names. I told you before not to call me names."

As Renee negotiated the crowded hall, Charlotte stormed up to her. "You were going to leave us out, weren't you!"

"What?"

"You were going to leave us out of your article on the ostracized."

"It's not about that exactly. It's more on—"

"I saw you talking to those LD geeks."

"Oh, that's nice, Charlotte."

"There's more gays and lesbians than there are retards, but you were going to blow us off, weren't you?"

"I guess I didn't think about it. But, you're right. You guys should be in the piece. So we'll find a time and—"

"We're like totally outside everything, okay? There's even quotas for blacks in medical school and stuff. Ever seen a quota for faggots and dykes?"

"They don't do quotas anymore."

"They *never* did it for us!"

"Look, take it easy. What do you want me to say exactly?"

"I don't know. Just don't leave us out of your stupid article."

Renee waved. "Arnie, can I talk to you a minute?"

"Oh, God: the gay perspective. What gave me away—my impeccable taste in clothes or those show tunes I can't help but hum?"

"I'm writing this piece on—"

"Losers. I heard."

"Rebels, outsiders, not losers. Just do me a favor, okay? And talk to me. If I don't get you guys in the paper, I'm afraid Charlotte's going to beat me up and make me wear a flannel shirt."

Arnie grinned. "Charlotte's a little hard to take. She's just come out, so she's carrying the banner."

"You're not?"

"I've known who I was since I was eleven. Bannerwise, I've been there, carried that."

"Do you think you're engaged in an intense self-exploration? Do you think you're challenging cultural values?"

"God, you're a hoot."

"Well, you know what I mean."

"Renee, do you think being gay is all that different from being straight?"

"I don't know. I guess I do."

Arnie shifted his biology book from one hand to the other. "Do you get depressed sometimes?"

"Sure."

"Me too. Do you get anxious?"

"Yeah."

"Me too. Ever wonder what we're all here for or if there's a god or why nice people get cancer and total bastards don't?"

"Sure."

"Everybody does. Who's your favorite movie star?"

Renee shrugged. "Brad Pitt, I guess."

Arnie looked up as the bell rang. "Me too. So why aren't we friends? We're really a lot alike."

Renee walked beside Bobby, talking a mile a minute. "Did you know that more than half the people in prison have attention deficit? They can't concentrate in school, so teachers call them troublemakers. Pretty soon they're self-medicating with caffeine or grass or speed and then—"

Bobby took hold of her arm. "Where'd you learn all this crap?"

"From William."

"Willard saw you two talking again. He said that geek was all over you."

"That's crazy. All I did was check some stuff for my—"

"I want you to stop writing that thing, Renee. I mean it. I never see you anymore, and when I do, all you care about is some dork you just interviewed."

"I'm almost done. Just one or two more."

Bobby turned, loomed over her, and shook his head. "I want you to stop now. We talked about this, remember? I'm not supposed to get upset before a game, and this crap is upsetting me."

Renee pulled away from him. "I don't like you telling me what I can and can't do."

"If I get upset and we lose the game, it'll be your fault."

"God, I know everything you're gonna say before you say it."

Bobby turned and slammed the nearest locker with his forearm.

Renee just shook her head. "I knew you were gonna do that too."

"Hi." Renee looked down at the three girls who were leaning together like conspirators. "Can I talk to you guys? I'm doing a piece about kids who don't usually get in the paper. Okay if I sit down?"

Chana cocked her head. "No, stand there so you can like totally condescend to us."

Debra waved to Renee. "Don't pay any attention to her. She just got her belly button pierced and it's all infected."

Molly nudged Chana. "Show her, girl."

"Get away. I'm all flabby. Look at Miss Perfect here. How many sit-ups do you do?"

"The piece isn't about me."

"Tell us, or we ain't none of us talkin'."

Renee sighed. "A couple hundred."

"Lord, makes me tired to think about it."

Renee slipped into an empty chair and opened her notebook. "What's it like having a baby and still being in high school?"

"Well, cut right to the chase."

"One thing I learned talking to people this week is no BS, okay?"

"That's cool."

"So?"

The three girls looked at one another. "Well, it's hard," Chana said finally. "When my grandma can't baby-sit, I can't come to school. Without school, I'm in more trouble than I am now."

"Do you guys ever go out on dates and stuff?"

All three shook their heads. "No time," said Chana.

"Not interested," Debra said.

Molly blushed. "I'm interested, but all guys want is to do the nasty. They think 'cause I did it at least once I'm just gonna fall on the nearest bed."

"What do you want to do after you graduate?"

Chana grinned. "I want to sit on the beach and have people give me money. But that position has apparently already been filled 'cause I never see it up on the Job Board."

"My sister started at Macy's part-time. Now she's an assistant buyer. I could do that."

Molly said, "My people make soap and go to craft fairs. Lot of single mothers in that business."

"Do you have pictures of your babies?"

"Not for no school newspaper, we don't."

Renee closed her notebook. "No, no. Just for me to look at."

Chana got hers out first.

"Oh, my God. She's precious."

"Yeah, well, let me find the one with the poopy diaper in it. You won't think she's so precious then." Chana had just finished laughing when she looked down at her T-shirt. "Oh, man. I'm leakin' again." She turned to Renee. "What's wrong with this picture? You're not supposed to leak milk on your Gap T-shirt. You wear a Gap T-shirt, you're supposed to be dancin' at a cookout and bein' all happy."

Renee, Debra, and Molly watched her head for the girls' rest room.

"She's all right," said Molly. "She just doesn't want to give up bein' seventeen. Now me. . . ." She tugged on the waistband of her stretch pants. "I settle for bein' comfortable."

"Are you guys sorry for the way things turned out?"

"I'm not sorry I've got my baby. No way am I sorry for that."

"I'm sorry I was stupid," Molly said. "Seems like boys'll say anything to . . . you know."

Renee reached for her beeper and turned it off.

Molly frowned. "Bobby's beepin' you from across the room?"

"Don't look at him."

"I'm already lookin' at him. He's got his cell phone to his ear."

Debra shook her head. "He's got you on a short leash, girlfriend. Is he worth it?"

Molly leaned in. "Yeah, what's he like in bed?"

Renee leaned back. "Are you kidding?"

Debra grinned. "No, she's not kidding. Give it up."

Renee looked around, then leaned in until her forehead almost touched theirs. "It takes about a minute and then he watches ESPN."

The three girls were still laughing when Chana sat down wearing a clean shirt. "So we're all friends now? We're comin' over your house, right? Hang with you and Bobby?"

Renee stood up and wiped at her eyes with the back of one hand, she'd laughed so hard. "One more question, okay? What did you all want to do or be before you were moms?"

Chana volunteered. "I didn't have no plans to speak of. So life sort of imposed itself on me, you know what I'm sayin'?"

Debra said, "I used to look at the maps in geography, okay? I liked the names—Somaliland, Thailand—and I thought maybe I'd like to go there, look at all those major exports piled on the dock."

"Well, this," said Molly, "is gonna sound funny comin' from somebody who got all those D's in English, but I always felt like I had something to say. Something kind of urgent, you know? Now it's just gonna have to wait."

The next day at lunch Renee walked into the cafeteria and sat down beside Bobby. "I'm taking a little vacation," she said.

"From what?"

"From everything. I want to think about some stuff."

"Like what?" He reached for her hand; she pulled away.

"I always thought I was like at the center of everything, you know? You and I and maybe ten other people: sports, school paper, yearbook staff, prom committee, all that stuff."

"Well, yeah. We are."

Renee shook her head. "No. It's not like that. They're not revolving around us. The truth is we're totally outside everybody else in this room."

Bobby looked baffled. "So?"

"You know those people you keep calling geeks and freaks and losers? Well, I like some of them."

"What are you talkin' about?"

She laid the beeper right in front of him. "Don't call me for a while, okay?"

"If you go out with that retard William, I swear to God I'll kill him."

"I'm not going out with anybody, okay? I'm going to read this book about outsiders. I'm going to sit in my room to think."

"You're nuts, you know that? Pretty soon you're gonna *be* one of those outsiders."

Renee stood up. She looked around the crowded, noisy room. Chana waved at her, William turned the page of his book, Arnie carried a tray with four yogurts.

I could sit anyplace in this cafeteria, she thought. I could even sit by myself.

Ron Koertge

Readers are sure to find colorful characters, a good amount of humor, and unusual situations in the novels of Ron Koertge. Although it's been some years since Ron was a teenager, he has a keen ear for realistic teenage dialogue and a sharp memory of how teenagers struggle with peer pressure, identity, sexual feelings, and insecurity. After enjoying this story, you might want to check out one or more of Koertge's award-winning novels: *Where the Kissing Never Stops; The Arizona Kid; The Boy in the Moon; Mairposa Blues; The Harmony Arms; Tiger, Tiger, Burning Bright; Confess-O-Rama;* and *The Heart of the City.*

The American Library Association has identified *The Arizona Kid* as one of the 100 Best of the Best Books for Young Adults published between 1967 and 1992. And the New York Public Library includes *Tiger, Tiger, Burning Bright* on its list of the 100 Best Children's Books; it was also named a Blue Ribbon Book by the *Bulletin for the Center of Children's Books,* a Bank Street Child Study Children's Book Committee Children's Book of the Year, a YALSA Best Book for Young Adults, and a Judy Lopez Memorial Award Honor Book.

In addition to writing novels and short stories for teenagers, Ron Koertge is a poet, a writing teacher at the city college in Pasadena, California, and a member of the faculty at Vermont College, where he teaches in the MFA in Writing for Children residency program.

His most recent collection of poems has been published under the title *Geography of the Forehead*. Koertge's newest novel, *The Brimstone Journals,* differs from his previous works in two ways: It is darker than his usual laugh-out-loud stories and is written in verse.

Great Expectations

M. E. Kerr

*Brian is such a wimp at school that the kids call him Mousey.
But after he meets Onondaga John, he's determined to show
everyone he isn't a loser. Can he?*

"HELLO, SON."

"Hi there!" I don't think he noticed that I'd stopped
calling him Dad. Not just because he wasn't my dad, but
because I wished with all my heart he was. I wished I'd
never become involved in this masquerade, and yet if I
hadn't, I never would have *met* Onondaga John.

It was a warm, early spring day, surprising in upstate
New York, where we often have snow up to our down-
stairs windows in March.

We sat in the prison visiting room. This was our third
meeting. The first had been at Thanksgiving. The second
at Christmas.

John Klee's face was lit by the few bars of sun that came through the high windows in the place. He had deep blue eyes, the color of his uniform. He told me once there was a saying: *True blue will never stain.* It meant that a truly noble heart will never disgrace itself . . . but it also referred to the blue aprons worn by butchers, which wouldn't show bloodstains.

"Johnny, today I want to tell you something I've never mentioned. Make yourself comfortable because there's a story attached."

"When isn't there a story?" I said with a smile. "Go ahead, sir."

He loved to talk about his life before Redmond, as though the young man he had once been was now understood by a gentler, wiser elder. He talked of his mistakes, some of them what he called "whoppers."

"I had no patience, Johnny, that was my one big flaw. I wanted everything right away." He'd said that both times. He said, "I don't hold that against myself, though. Growing up, I was the poor kid, the one whose family got the charity box from the Rotary Club every year. Grown up, I was a show-off—never drove a black car if I could get one fire-engine red. My wheels squealed around corners and my horn played 'Sweet Talkin' Guy.'"

He didn't tell me sob stories, nor did he make himself the hero of his tales. He just wanted me to know him. He wanted to know me too. Not really me—he'd never know *me*. But he wanted to know his son.

My real name is Brian Moore. I am Millie Moore's kid, one of these single-parent children. So in the beginning it sounded like fun to pretend I was Onondaga John's son.

My mother's bed-and-breakfast, called the Blue Moon, specializes in the families of men locked up in Redmond Prison, right in our downtown.

When you cater to a crowd of women (mostly) whose brothers or husbands or fathers are doing nickels and dimes, you get to know them. Onondaga John is doing two quarters, and of that fifty-year sentence he's served only sixteen years.

We call Mrs. Klee, his wife, Polly Posh, because there is something posh about her, something glamorous— even though, as she likes to say, her days of Concorde flights and mansions, silk sheets and chauffeurs, are over. She is a forty-eight-year-old con's wife. Her rich family want nothing to do with her. Neither does her son, the real Johnny. He moved in with his grandparents when he was eight years old. Now, at Oxford House, he tells his prep school pals that his dad is dead.

For a long while Onondaga John didn't want anything to do with his son either. He was ashamed of himself, and uncertain about how the boy felt toward him. Early in his sentence Polly had said something about not wanting to bring a little kid to Redmond Prison, not wanting to have him see his father that way. Onondaga John thought there was a possibility she'd lied to their boy, maybe said he was on some secret mission far away . . . maybe even said he was dead. It wasn't uncommon for prisoners' wives to keep the truth from their kids.

Onondaga John didn't even ask to see pictures of

Johnny Jr. Let Polly bring up the boy the way she thought best.

He asked her if Johnny needed anything, if everything was okay with him—general references, but nothing specific. Polly guessed Onondaga John was too proud to face a little tyke walking through those iron doors, calling out "Daddy." Not *his* son! Leave well enough alone.

Polly was just as glad he felt that way. She never had to tell her husband that the boy had turned into Little Lord-It-Over-Everyone. She never had to tell Onondaga John that his son claimed to be fatherless.

Then came the fatal day when Onondaga John told Polly he'd like to meet his son. "Isn't he around sixteen now?"

"Yes." Polly told my mother she was thinking right then and there that *I* was around sixteen too.

"Does he know about me, Polly?"

"Yes."

"Bring him along next time. I'm not planning to become a daddy to him suddenly. I just want to see him."

"Sure," Polly said.

That night at the Blue Moon, Polly asked my mother and me, "What would it hurt if Brian visited him, said he was his son?"

"Well, Brian," said my mother, "here's your chance to be an actor. Here's your chance to prove to everyone at that school you're the Tom Hanks of Redmond, not some flop!"

"He can't *tell* anyone he's doing it!" said Polly. "And who said he was a flop?"

"That's what they think of him," said my mother. "Ask him."

"Why do they think that, Brian?" Polly asked me.

"Not every kid comes across as interesting. *I* don't." That was putting it mildly. I didn't "come across" at all, except as El Nerdo.

"This might make you *feel* interesting," Polly said, "even if you can't talk about it."

I said, "It'd be a change anyway."

I thought the main thing would be seeing inside Redmond. You live in a prison city your whole life never knowing what's behind those walls. You see the guys going and coming on the buses in and out of Redmond. Going with a birdcage and the shiny new suit the state pays for. Coming, manacled to a plainclothesman, not wanting to look you in the eye.

But the main thing didn't turn out to be Redmond Prison. It was Onondaga John himself. Right away he asked me how I felt about things, and he told me how *he* did. He said his favorite author was Charles Dickens and one of his favorite books was *Great Expectations*. What do you like to read, he wanted to know, and whose music do you like? What do you want to be someday? "An *actor?*" he said. "Hey! Hey!" he said, grinning at me, looking as pleased as though I'd just unlocked the front gate and said "You're free."

I'd never had an adult male interested in me unless it was a guidance counselor wanting to know why my fingernails were chewed down to the quick, or why I couldn't stop rubbing away my eyebrows.

I'm okay when I'm at the Blue Moon. I belong there, setting up the chips for the poker games, listening to old Mrs. Resnick cry that her hubby no sooner gets out than he goes right back in, answering the rattle of bells at the front door, always eager to see if it's someone new, someone whose relative we've seen on Court TV.

Everyone there likes me too. Everyone knows I'll sneak a peanut butter sandwich to them late at night. I'll let the cats up the back stairs to sleep with those who need a little fur and purr around their necks. I'll get them thrillers or romance books from the library with my card. I'll watch the spooky stuff on TV with them in our parlor, and I can sit in for card games too. Bridge, poker, and gin.

Follow me out of the Blue Moon, down two blocks and over three, and you've seen me land in enemy territory: Redmond High School.

Mousey Moore, on the short side with thin brown hair and bird legs, arms just as skinny.

At the Blue Moon I babble and crack jokes and listen and hum.

In that puke-yellow brick building with the flagpole out front, I am duh. I scurry down the halls like the mousey they've named me. Not even mouse. I am littler. My whiskers bristle with fear. My nostrils quiver. Inside, everything trembles.

"Hey, Mousey, did you bring a cheese sandwich for lunch?" Someone has tossed an empty Coke can at the back of my head.

"Did the mousey bring cheese for himself? Did you, Mousey?"

"Yis." I can't even make it sound like yes. It hisses out of me between chattering teeth: *Yisss*.

"Is the cat after you, Mousey?" I feel a sneaker press down on the back of my shoe.

"Nip." For nope—nip, and I skitter down the hall to get away, oh-oh, not in the boys', it'll be worse in there. Try by your locker. Just open the door and hide by your locker.

But there is no way for someone like me to hide at school.

I hide in my head, fantasizing that I've grown tall and strong enough to fight them. Or suddenly so unbelievably handsome and amusing they all long to be my friend.

I pray for days when something *big* is going on in the town or the world, taking their minds off me.

Now Onondaga John was at the end of his story, which was about his courtship of Polly Posh, how he adored her, and how frightened he was of Mr. Pullman, her father: rich and powerful, six foot three, with a booming voice. Pullman would look down his nose at John Klee and say things like "Don't wear brown shoes again, fellow. It's not a man's color."

"You don't know what that's like, do you, Johnny? To be scorned. Polly tells me you have lots of friends at your fancy school. What's its name?"

"Oxford House, sir."

"Yes. Your grandfather Pullman went there, and his father too."

"Yes, sir."

"Do you admire the Pullmans, Johnny?"

"Not really, sir." Not from what I'd heard about them! Polly said Johnny'd become so spoiled living there. He instructed the maids to remove all magazine inserts before putting them in his room. He only wore a terry-cloth robe once, then threw it out and grabbed a new one from the shelf in his bathroom. The entire Pullman family were wastrels, said Polly—greedy and ungiving.

Onondaga John said, "I was afraid you'd come under their influence, since you're their only grandchild. I'm glad you stuck with your mother!"

That was when he told me he was going to see that I received $240,000.

I swallowed hard. "But where would you get that much money, sir?"

"Let's say from a partner of mine, Johnny."

I had never asked him about the last bank robbery, though I did know it was the first time he had worked with partners. Before that he always went solo, and only robbed banks in Onondaga County, upstate New York.

There were three robbers in the Salina Bank robbery. I did know that one turned state witness and claimed Onondaga John shot the cop. Polly swore he never had, he *wouldn't*, it wasn't in him to kill anyone. Steal, yes! Kill, uh-uh!

The third man had apparently taken off with the loot from the heist.

"Johnny? You look slightly reluctant. It's not dirty money, Johnny. It doesn't belong to people. I've never robbed *people*. I've robbed banks, and banks reimburse depositors. Insurance is a business like any other, with its risks and gains. They bet someone like me won't come along. I bet someone like them won't be prepared when I do."

"I never thought of it that way." I'd never thought of it at all.

"This is just another little mystery story, Johnny." Sometimes at the end of a story he'd say that, then add, "Life is mysterious. You don't know that yet, but you'll see."

"It's very hard for me to believe," I told him.

"I plan to give you thirty thousand dollars a year for eight years," said Onondaga John. "Your first payment will come to the Blue Moon, in cash, in six months."

My mouth must have fallen open; my eyes must have been round with amazement.

"Don't say anything, Johnny, just listen. It will be yours to do with as you please. I like the way you've turned out. I trust you, Son. Unlike me, you have a noble heart you will *not* disgrace."

I don't know about a noble heart. Do you know what I thought I'd do first with the money? I would hire a drama student from Redmond University, where theater was featured. He would be big and tough looking, able to handle himself in any circumstance. I would buy a Saab convertible for him to drive. We would get some Redmond University coeds to accompany us. We would appear at all the games together, at the dances, at Pizza Palace, all the places I never went, fearing the bullies would be there too.

I would no longer be Mousey Moore. Moose, maybe. The Moose.

* * *

"We can't take that money," said my mother. "Brian, what could you be thinking of? Stolen money? It's bad luck, honey!"

"He didn't offer it to *us*, Mom. He offered it to me. I can take it." I gave her Onondaga John's explanation about insurers being businessmen, about risks attached to business.

"Malarkey!" she said. "That's how Onondaga John got where he is!"

That night after the poker game Polly said she was going back the next afternoon.

"Then send us an E-mail that Johnny's been hit by a two-ton truck," said my mother. "We are ready to end this charade."

"Not me," I said. "I'm not ready."

"I can't say that I blame you, Brian," Polly said. "Now I understand why John wanted to meet his son. He told me what he's planning. Better you than the real Johnny! And I'll expect to be a nonpaying lodger after you get your first installment."

"If that money comes to this house, it'll go right back!" said my mother.

"Go right back where?" Polly said. "Apparently the third man is dying, and he's already put the cash somewhere in John's name."

"We won't have any trouble getting someone to take it away," said my mother. "Particularly someone in navy blue with a silver badge."

"That's a lot of money," said Polly.

"You keep it if you love having stolen money so much," said my mother.

Polly gave me a wink. She said, "What boy couldn't use some new clothes and music and something like a little Saab to get around in?"

"Convertible," I said. "A Saab convertible."

By the time Polly left, she had jollied my mother into thinking about it.

But my mother did ask me, "What kind of values do you have that you think it's important to have new clothes, new music, and a new Saab?"

"Convertible," I said. "A new Saab convertible."

"What kind of values are those?"

"Teenage values," I said.

"Do they teach you that at school?"

"They don't have to," I said. "It's our job to know it."

Suddenly, back at school, this girl who was head of the drama club asked me if I would be in a play.

She can see the change in me already, I decided. I had a suspicion there was a new spring to my step and I might even have grown an inch since the thought that $240,000 could be mine . . . soon.

Polly had kissed me good-bye and said hang in there, we'll work on Mom. I somehow could not believe my mother, upright and honest as she is, would really not go to sleep thinking of things we could have with $30,000 a year to spend. We needed a computer, since ours from the early eighties had finally crashed, and we needed a third bathroom, and we needed new poker chips. We were not unneedy at the Blue Moon.

I told the President of Redmond High School Players Club that of course I would accept a role in the play.

How many times had I tried out for parts that always went to someone else?

Making myself sound no more excited than I imagined Leonardo DiCaprio might be, offered a movie role, I asked what the play was called.

"What You Really Are Is What You Don't Eat," she said. "It's an original comedy about food fads."

"What's my part?" I knew I wouldn't be the lead. It didn't matter. It was a beginning.

"You'll be a rabbit. You know how your nostrils vibrate sometimes, Mousey?"

So there was *not* a new spring to my step, new growth, or anything new to accompany the visions I had of cars and travel and college campuses spread out over lush green hills, some sweaters (cashmere), pants, coats, toss a cap in, keep going, keep going.

I was still not quite human by the standards at RHS. But I had progressed from a rodent to a hare.

That afternoon on my way from school I was tripped, pushed, made to flush like a toilet on the circular cement walk, and warned that life was short for shorties. Just another day in Paradise.

Ah, but then, as Onondaga John liked to say, Fate frolicked into the picture. Walking along Genesee Street, I saw the spanking-new Marshall Sylvester Saab Center. In the window was a beige convertible with beige leather seats.

I made a casual entrance—just slipped inside, you might say—and sidled over for a look-see.

"You're the kid from the Blue Moon," Mr. Sylvester said. "I remember you used to come into my showroom on Jefferson Avenue and say you just wanted to have a look-see. I don't spend the day in a suit and tie to talk to little squirts about cars!"

"I'm not looking for myself. I'm looking for Johnny Klee Jr. Ever hear of him? He's inherited a fortune."

"No, I never heard of him. You *are* the kid from the Blue Moon, though, aren't you?"

"So what? I'm not always going to be the kid from the Blue Moon. My friend, Johnny Klee, goes to Oxford House, in Boston, Mass. And he would prefer to have brown leather seats in his convertible, not those beige ones."

"Yeah, yeah. Tell him to come in. Who did he inherit the fortune from?"

"His father."

"Klee? From around here?"

"Did I say from around here?"

"Tell him brown leather seats will take eight weeks."

"We'll wait."

"Yeah, yeah. How's business at the Blue Moon? With all these dope addicts being sent up for grand theft and manslaughter, your mother must be rich."

"The one who's rich," I said, "is my buddy, Johnny Klee Jr."

There are people you just can't impress, and that seemed to be the case with Marshall Sylvester. I slunk out of the showroom trying to whistle nonchalantly, telling myself: *So what!*

* * *

I couldn't go to Redmond Prison just anytime at all. I had to wait for Polly to come to town. But my thoughts were on Onondaga John. When I wasn't thinking of new things I would buy for myself, I would find something somewhere that John Klee would like: a tin of those Altoid peppermints he favored; Old English aftershave; a rhyming dictionary, since he told me he wrote poetry. I even found him a leather-bound copy of *Great Expectations*. It was an interesting story for me to read at this point in my life, for it was about a boy who also had "great expectations" of money. I was going to be a grateful and attentive recipient. I was going to be a son.

"Is Mrs. Moore in?" the guy said.

"She'll be right back," I said, looking him over, figuring he was probably in Redmond to see a brother or a father, his first time, shy about saying why he was there. Someone had given him the address of the Blue Moon, even though we were known to favor female clients. We liked help in the kitchen, clean bathrooms, anything but sports on the big TV in the parlor—and other things along those lines that a male clientele did not guarantee.

"Sit down," I said. "You don't have to stand."

"I like to stand," he said. He was one of those. How dare *I* suggest a course of action *he* should take?

I slung my schoolbooks on the couch in our parlor and took a good look at this long young man. The teeniest, tiniest gold stud in his left ear, black hair, probably shoulder length, tied back with a bit of leather.

"If you're planning to stay here," I said, "I can sign you in."

"I don't know if I'm staying or not. I'd like to know about the visiting hours at the . . . ahem . . . um . . . prison here in town."

"Tomorrow you can visit between noon and three," I said.

"Then I'm forced to stay, I guess."

"I'll sign you in," I said, crossing to my mother's small desk. "Your name?"

"John Pullman," he said.

"John . . . *Pullman*." Of course. He had taken his grand-parents' name.

"I want to stay on a smoke-free floor, in a room with a view and a comfortable chair with arms, a private bath, and a double bed."

If I had imagined in my wildest dreams how the real Johnny would look and act, it would be exactly as the real Johnny looked and acted. Preppies always seem more confident, and feel free to order you around.

"Another thing." I found out this was a favorite way for him to begin sentences. "Can you tell me anything about Marshall Sylvester?"

"He's the Saab dealer here," I said.

"Yes, so he announced when he called Oxford House looking for Johnny Klee. I haven't been called that since I was eight years old! When it came over the intercom I about had a duck!"

He looked down at me and his lips tipped into a snide, lopsided grin. "And you must be the kid from the Blue Moon who said I'd prefer brown leather seats to beige ones in my new convertible."

"The beige are harder to keep clean," I said, everything

inside me sinking to my shoes, heart pounding, nervous breakdown suggestions throughout my terminals.

"Another thing," he barked, "what do you know about my father leaving me money?"

"I was just kidding," I croaked. People really do croak in dire circumstances. I learned that.

"What do you know about that old jailbird? What do you know about the third man?" He bent down so that he could look me in the eye. "And how does my mother fit into this picture?"

What would be the ending to this story? Onondaga John might ask, if he was telling it. And is this a story about who gets the money, or is it a story about what the thought of getting the money can do?

Perhaps it's both. As Onondaga John would point out, there are many levels to the best stories, and in life there are levels galore!

The thought of getting the money did not make much of a dent on Polly Posh, though she was curious about where it came from.

My mother reacted to the thought of getting the money with hostile threats.

Marshall Sylvester went to his computer as he thought of getting the money, and was able to locate a Saab dealer in Mattituck, New York, with a convertible, in stock, complete with brown leather seats. He made a phone call to Oxford House.

The thought of anyone else getting the money brought the real Johnny to Redmond, finally, to meet his father.

No one but the fly on the wall knows what was said between the two. It was the first and last visit.

Now me. The thought of getting the money made me strut away from duh and yissss and nip for whatever brief time. True, I was propelled by borrowed glory, and there are finer places than the Marshall Sylvester Saab Showroom to boast in . . . and a more receptive audience than the cynical and sarcastic Sylvester himself. But I don't take that blame, for I was new to the promise of a windfall—impatient and flawed.

I *did* write a story about it, in the style of Onondaga John: Sit back, relax, and I'll tell you a mistake I made—a whopper!

"The Fool in the Saab Showroom" was its title.

It was the only A+ that I ever received in any subject, and across the top my English teacher wrote: "How interesting! What an imagination!"

"Hey, Mousey!" a kid yelled at me as I hurried home from the trenches and minefields of RHS. "Where'd you steal that story from?"

Then there was a chorus: *Is there any cure for poor Mouse Moore?*

Instead of provoking respect in my predators, I inspired them to reach a new creative height: *rhyming.*

One day there was a postcard on my bed, where Mother left all mail: on people's beds. It said:

> Thanks for the look at your story, Brian! You're
> a better actor than a writer, in my opinion, but

then I saw you act three times, and this is the only story of yours I've read.

If it's good enough to be included in your school literary magazine that should tell you something.

Out of our biggest difficulties, we make our little songs.

Do I mind that you put me in a story, you ask? It is the only justification I can think of for deceiving me. So I don't mind. You wouldn't have had a story without me.

I gave you a lot of material, so in a sense, you have great expectations, after all. (Thanks for the book etc.)

Here's my advice to you: Use it all. Keep on writing. Use everything that comes your way.

Farewell, J.K.

No one I know ever found out what became of the money from the third man, not even Polly Posh.

John Klee would say, "This is just another little mystery story. Life is mysterious. You don't know that yet, but you'll see."

And of course those schoolmates of mine are right: There is no cure for poor Mouse Moore.

They will always be coming after me.

They are what I have come to expect.

M. E. Kerr

For more than thirty years Marijane Meaker has been writing award-winning novels and short stories for teenagers under the name of M. E. Kerr. Her first novel, *Dinky Hocker Shoots Smack!,* helped define contemporary literature for young adults. As one of the genre's leading authors, Kerr is the recipient of the Margaret A. Edwards Award for lifetime accomplishments and the 1999 Knickerbocker Award for Juvenile and Young Adult Literature from the New York Public Library Association. Long Island University awarded her an honorary doctorate in 1996.

The idea for "Great Expectations" goes back to when Meaker was a teenager living in Auburn, New York, where there was a prison and many homes where the families of prisoners stayed. She says, "We were always very aware of the prison . . . and I was always wondering about those inside."

Ever willing to take chances, she has dealt with a variety of unusual topics in her novels, including teenage soap opera stars in *I'll Love You When You're More Like Me,* teenage dwarfs in *Little Little,* religious experiences in *What I Really Think of You,* the Gulf War in *Linger,* rock stars and homosexuality in *"Hello," I Lied,* lesbian teenagers in *Deliver Us from Evie,* AIDS in *Night Kites,* and the horror of the Holocaust in *Gentlehands. Gentlehands* has been identified by the American Library Association as one of the 100 Best of the Best Books for Young Adults published betwen 1967 and 1992. M. E. Kerr is also the author of a popular mystery-detective series for teens starring John Fell: *Fell, Fell Back,* and *Fell Down.*

Kerr's most recent novels for teens include *What Became of Her,* a story about an eccentric old woman and the impact three teenagers have on her life, and *Slap Your Sides,* about a young Quaker boy whose older brother becomes a conscientious objector during World War II in a small town in Pennsylvania.

More information is available about M. E. Kerr and her books on www.columbia.edu/~msk28/.

Shortcut

Nancy Werlin

If you feel superior to most of your classmates but you're no longer part of the "in" group at school, where does that leave you? Lacey finds herself in this position . . . and then learns something that makes her feel even worse.

THURSDAY AFTERNOON. Last period. Eighth-grade science lab. Ms. Davies was supervising the cleaning of pipettes and beakers, but Lacey had already washed her stuff. She sat with her hands tightly entwined in her lap, her jacket on, her eye on the clock. She was silent; she had no one to talk to anyway.

She was plotting her route out.

She wouldn't run; she never ran. It was undignified. And—conspicuous. She couldn't afford that, especially not today.

Lacey had to be at the shortcut in time to head off Catrine. She'd tell her to take the long way home. For today, at least, that ought to make her safe from Will Brennerman and his friends.

Will Brennerman. Oh, God. How was it possible? And you couldn't tell anyone, that would just make it worse—worse for Catrine, and probably for Lacey too. Nobody would believe anything bad of Will anyway. He'd smile, those white teeth would gleam . . . But how could Lacey warn Catrine without risking her own safety? She'd be seen! It was risky, it was impossible—

Lacey suddenly saw that she'd picked up a pencil and was clutching it in her right fist. As if her hand belonged to a stranger, she stared at its white knuckles. Then, slowly, she forced her fingers open. The pencil dropped onto the lab table with a small clatter. It wasn't even sharpened. It was harmless.

Useless.

After today Catrine would just have to look out for herself. This was all Lacey was going to do for her. A warning. And it was a lot too. Nobody could expect more.

Two minutes, said the clock.

Actually, Lacey didn't have to warn Catrine. She could change her mind. She could linger late at school; avoid the whole thing. Pretend she didn't know. Why not? Catrine and Lacey had never liked each other. Lacey didn't owe Catrine Messer anything; really she didn't. It had been many years since— And it had been Rhonda who'd started it, not Lacey. and it had been fourth grade, for God's sake!

Lacey's stomach made an audible noise. The girl who sat next to her cast her a look of disdain. Lacey flinched.

Already today, she'd missed one opportunity to warn Catrine. She'd tried to tell herself she didn't believe it; that what she'd overheard Rhonda saying, insinuating, in the girls' room couldn't possibly be true.

But she'd known better. True, Lacey didn't know Catrine well, and couldn't judge what she might or might not do. But she knew Rhonda. Oh, yes, Lacey knew Rhonda Harris.

As if it were yesterday rather than more than four years ago, Lacey could see Rhonda tossing Catrine's cupcake box on the sidewalk. Laughing. "Come on, Lacey, smash it!" she'd said, and jumped forward. And then Lacey could see her own small yellow-sneakered foot rising into the air. And then stomping downward on top of Catrine's chocolate birthday cupcakes. Left, left. Right, right.

Here, now, in science lab, Lacey felt her legs tremble. Involuntarily, she glanced down at her feet.

Okay. Fine. Fine, then.

When the bell rang, Lacey would run. She would intercept Catrine before Catrine started to take the shortcut home. She would warn her.

This once.

Lacey watched the clock. She swallowed the lump in her throat. Fifteen seconds. Fourteen. Thirteen . . .

In good weather Lacey always took the shortcut. Despite its steep downhill grade through the woods, despite the mud and rocks that made the descent into the ravine tricky, it was irresistible. Not only did it take a full seven minutes off her walk home, but it was *safe*—safe in the way that mattered. The fact was, the only other kids from Lacey's large suburban neighborhood who used the shortcut were also . . . also . . .

Also what? Like Lacey? Lacey hated that thought. She wasn't like the other shortcutters. You only had to look at her—at them—to see that.

It wasn't only Catrine whom Lacey objected to. Catrine was the definition of unacceptable, of course, with her acne wasteland of a face. Her hunched shoulders. Her history of always being the one everybody laughed at, despised. But that fat nerd Quentin DeSantos wasn't much better. Quentin thought he had to show how smart he was, all the time. So much for intelligence.

Then there was stupid, hulking Saul Blum. Please. Saul had stayed back—was it twice? In another sense, though, he was lucky. At least people left him alone. On a few occasions, in the privacy of her heart, Lacey would have swapped anything for Saul's size.

And then, rounding out the Five Freaks, came Joey and Josie Umanita. The big joke about the Umanita twins was that you had to take their different sexes on faith. They were the same height and breadth, they had identical shoulder-length haircuts, their features were somehow both masculine and feminine, and both of them wore bib overalls, plaid shirts, and work boots every single day. "One of them's a sex change operation waiting to happen—but which one?" Rhonda had quipped, early this year. Everyone had laughed. "Maybe both," someone else had added snidely—wait, had it been Will Brennerman? Yes, Lacey thought it had. And then he'd gone on to say other things about the Umanitas. Things that made your skin crawl, even in remembering.

At the time Lacey had smiled along with everyone else, even though no one was paying attention to her. Even though she was, by then, an invisible person at school. She'd smiled because she had to at least try. She'd thought things might change. She still thought so. Hoped so. Somebody might suddenly see that there was nothing weird about Lacey after all; that Rhonda had made a mistake at the beginning of the year, dumping Lacey the way she had, saying those things about her, freezing her out. Leaving her alone.

Yes, Lacey might belong again, if she was careful. Belong somewhere. It was possible. And even if that didn't happen . . . then at least, if Lacey was careful, nothing worse would happen to her.

She could tolerate the ordinary daily stuff. The hard shoves in the back in the corridors, when she didn't dare turn to see who'd hit her. Overhearing the endless invitations and plans in which she wasn't included. The terrible loneliness of the lunchroom. Even the gum in her hair—after all, that had only happened once. She could tolerate all of it, she had decided, so long as she knew there would be nothing worse.

Which there wouldn't be. As long as she was careful.

As long as she didn't offend anyone.

Bell!

Lacey was the first one out of science lab. She kept her head down and moved, moved. Past the blue lockers. Down the staircase. Through the double doors. Into the west wing, and down another flight of stairs. And okay, finally, there was the door closest to the shortcut. Another minute and she'd be outside. Then she could sprint. Oh, God. Oh, God.

If only she hadn't had to go to the bathroom so desperately that morning. If only she hadn't overheard Rhonda.

"She stabbed Will in the arm with a pencil! Can you imagine?" Rhonda had said. "I mean, what about lead poisoning? That could have been *serious*."

Sitting in the last cubicle, with its broken door slightly ajar and her feet drawn up—the safe way to use the bathroom, when you had to, when you simply couldn't hold it—Lacey had tightened her arms around her knees and closed her eyes briefly. Rhonda, she'd thought. It had to be Rhonda cutting class at the only time I could sneak in here. Now I'll have to stay until after she leaves. I'll miss history. I'll get in trouble.

She'd snapped back to attention when the girl Rhonda had been speaking to—Lacey thought it was Alicia Stern—asked something.

"Oh, who cares?" Rhonda replied. "You know Will. He's always fooling around. Listen, whatever he did to her, she didn't have the right to *stab* him."

"Mm." Alicia appeared to agree. And after a moment, she'd added: "She's in my homeroom. And this morning? You won't believe it. She stood at the front of the room sharpening one pencil after another. An entire box! And Will was right there too. She didn't look at him. She just kept sharpening."

"Weird," Rhonda commented interestedly.

"*So* weird."

There'd been a pause. Then Rhonda had lowered her voice. "Alicia? Listen, I know something."

Almost against her will, Lacey strained to hear. Rhonda's voice had dropped again, and if Lacey hadn't known her so well, she might not have been able to make out any words at all.

But she did.

After school. Will's going to show that bitch to watch out who she stabs. She takes that route through the woods . . . Jase is going too, and Pete and Carl . . .

Lacey had hugged her knees harder. *Show that bitch. Show that bitch.* She'd tried, quietly, to breathe despite the new, huge, lump in her throat.

Who? What bitch? Although at least it wasn't Lacey, and that was all that mattered, really.

And then Rhonda said, "You know, I'd kill myself if I were her. She's the ugliest girl in the entire school."

Lacey had known then. For several long seconds she ceased to breathe at all.

"In fact, when you think about it," Rhonda had added, "Catrine Messer would be better off dead."

The shortcut had always been safe. As she raced there, Lacey spared a moment for mourning. The shortcut would never be the same again, she knew. Catrine had ruined it. Ruined it for all of them.

Desperately, now, she wished she'd warned her earlier, after lunch. She could have, if she'd tried. Lacey had been yards away, but a gap in the crowd had let her see Catrine clearly. Catrine, in her thick makeup, wearing a short, tight skirt that defiantly displayed her gorgeous legs. She had a yogurt container and spoon in her left hand. And in her right she'd been clutching—a pencil. Maybe *the* pencil. Sharp, pointed.

Useless.

Yes, Lacey should have pushed her way through the crowd and warned Catrine then. She should have taken the risk of talking to her in public. It would have been better. It would have been safer than this.

Lacey prayed as she ran. Her book bag bounced against her side. Maybe Catrine wouldn't be there yet; maybe she could ask Quentin or Saul or the twins to pass on the message for her. Assuming they were there. Then Lacey herself could go home the long way, which was now safer than the shortcut—

Lacey stopped dead. The lump in her throat re-expanded. A few yards ahead, at the very top of the slope where the shortcut began, in plain sight of the school, stood Catrine. She was just . . . standing there.

Then she was looking straight at Lacey. Frowning a little. And, Lacey now saw, fat Quentin DeSantos was standing right next to her.

Odd. Lacey didn't think she'd seen Catrine and Quentin even speak before. All of the shortcutters— except of course the Umanitas—had always done the shortcut on their own. They weren't friends. They weren't a group. Each of them was alone.

Well, it wasn't Lacey's concern. Will Brennerman, his friends—*they* were a group. And they'd be in the woods somewhere, waiting. Or maybe they were coming this way now. Whichever, she needed to warn Catrine and then get away from here. She took the last few steps that brought her face-to-face with Catrine. She opened her mouth—

"What the hell are you doing here?" said Catrine.

Lacey hated Catrine again, suddenly, virulently. She

gritted her teeth. Too bad. She'd come here to warn her, and she would. "Listen. I wanted to tell you that I—I heard something—"

"Me too," interrupted Catrine. Her voice was almost bored. "I hear a lot. Get out of here, Lacey. Take the long way today. Go."

The long way? Did Catrine know? But if she did, what was she doing here? She ought to take the long way herself! "Catrine—"

"Yes," interrupted Quentin DeSantos. Oddly, his voice was suddenly almost gentle. "You should go now, Lacey."

Puzzled, Lacey gave him a glance. Was there something different about him? It didn't matter. There wasn't time. She turned quickly back toward Catrine and found she couldn't quite meet her eyes. It didn't matter. She spoke rapidly. "I'll go in a minute, okay? But first I just need to make sure you know not to take the shortcut today. I heard—I heard that Will Brennerman and some of his friends might—might be waiting for you." Lacey swallowed. There. She'd said it.

She dared to look at Catrine. Catrine's awful face was blank, expressionless. Not horrified; not surprised; not frightened. Or maybe that was the makeup. Well, fine. Lacey didn't need thanks. She took a step back, away. She turned.

And nearly collided with big Saul Blum. "Sorry," he mumbled. It was the first word Lacey had ever heard him utter. Her eyes nearly bugged out of her head. Against her will, she turned halfway back to watch incredulously as Saul walked right up to Catrine and said something else, something Lacey couldn't hear.

And then stood on Catrine's other side.

Three. Three of them now, three complete losers standing in plain view of anyone who might come along. And planning—what? To walk the shortcut together?

Did they think that would help? Had Quentin and Saul lost their minds? This was Will Brennerman! Three losers couldn't win against him, against all of Them. No matter how strong Saul was. Lacey knew. She knew; she had been one of Them. Once.

She had to get out of here, had to—

Why couldn't she move?

The Umanita twins brushed by Lacey. She wasn't surprised to see them. One of them said to her, uncertainly, "Lacey, are you, um, you know that Catrine needs . . . ?" She ignored the words. Suddenly Lacey hated the twins too. No matter what, they had each other.

They were looking at her now, all five of them. There was a question on every face except Catrine's. And meanwhile Lacey couldn't help it, she stared back. Her heart pumped wildly. She needed to leave.

The cupcakes. Lacey—Lacey had laughed. And Catrine had cried, and cried, and cried.

She wasn't crying now. She was staring at Lacey. She said, again, "Go, Lacey. Go." It was a command.

But Lacey couldn't seem to move. She wet her lips. She whispered, "What are you doing? What are you planning?"

One of the Umanitas spoke up then. Josie. You could tell from her voice, which was . . . almost kind. "We're taking the shortcut, Lacey. Like we always do. That's all."

"But," Lacey said feebly. "But they'll be waiting . . ." Her voice trailed off.

"We know," said Saul Blum.

"We're ready," said Quentin DeSantos.

There was a little silence.

"Go, Lacey," said Catrine again. "Go. Be safe." Now, for some reason, she didn't sound angry. For a minute Lacey didn't recognize the emotion in her voice. And then, suddenly, she did.

It was pity.

Lacey's face flamed. Pity! She couldn't stand it. Pity! After what she'd done, coming here, warning Catrine! Risking . . .

She turned sharply and began walking away. She kept her back perfectly straight. She *would* be safe. Unlike them. And she wouldn't be pitied! She wouldn't be pitied by that loser, that—that ugly—

She swallowed. That—that—that—

That brave, smart girl.

Those loyal, kind outcasts.

Abruptly, Lacey stopped walking. Her body, her entire brain, froze. And then . . .

We know.

We're ready.

It was as if she had woken up from a deep, poisoned sleep. Woken with knowledge. She clutched at her own arms. For a second she thought she would fall over. She had been blind. Blind, and stupid. She had understood nothing.

But now she did. Now she knew why the shortcut had been safe. And she knew something else too: They had *let* her use the shortcut.

They had let her be safe. When Rhonda had told everyone Lacey's most intimate fears; when Rhonda had labeled Lacey a pathetic, clingy loser; when, overnight, and for no reason except to feed Rhonda's feeling of power, Lacey's life had changed completely—they had let her be safe.

It couldn't be too late. She whirled around again to face the shortcut.

The other five had started down into the ravine. Josie had already disappeared from sight. And Saul, nearly. It was now or never, Lacey knew. Her heart was in her mouth. Now or never.

It was now.

"Wait!" she called. Then again, more urgently: "Wait! Catrine! Saul! Quentin! Josie! Joey!"

For a moment she thought they wouldn't respond. But then they turned back. Five pairs of eyes looked at Lacey across the distance between them.

Cautiously, she took a step forward. Then another, until she was almost directly in front of them. She fixed her eyes on Catrine's, and then moved them to each of the others', in turn. At last she returned her gaze to Catrine. She swallowed.

"Can I come?" Lacey asked. Her voice didn't crack after all. But she was caught off guard by the naked need that even she could hear in it. So she had to swallow again before she could add, strongly, and with all her heart:

"Please."

Nancy Werlin

A Massachusetts native and currently a resident of South Boston, Nancy Werlin has been employed as a technical writer for various software companies since graduating from Yale University. Although she decided to be a fiction writer at ten, it took two decades before she published her first novel, *Are You Alone on Purpose?* That story of two teenagers struggling with family problems, handicaps, and their own identity earned her high praise. The American Library Association chose it as a Quick Pick for Reluctant Readers and identified it as a Popular Paperback for young adults.

Her second and third novels—*The Killer's Cousin* and *Locked Inside*—are both psychological thrillers that not only keep readers in delicious suspense but go far beyond the usual mystery/adventure story in their examination of characters' motivations and interpersonal relations. Among its many honors, *The Killer's Cousin* received the 1999 Edgar Award for Best Young Adult Mystery; it was also named an ALA Best Book for Young Adults, an ALA Quick Pick, and a Teens' Top 10 Best Book Pick.

Werlin's story "Shortcut" was partly inspired by a personal experience. When she was in eighth grade and taking a shortcut through the woods, she overheard a girl from her neighborhood making vicious fun of a classmate. This was repeated for days. "I didn't want any trouble for myself, so I kept my mouth shut," she confesses. Not only did she feel ashamed of her silence, she says, but she also was surprised when a boy whom she thought little of spoke up in defense of the boy who was being harassed. "I've never forgotten that day and what I learned about myself," Werlin says. "It was a trigger for change in me."

You can find out more about Nancy Werlin by checking her website at www.world. std.com/~nwerlin.

Through a Window

Angela Johnson

Sometimes we think we know someone because we see him or her almost every day. Then something happens to make us realize we didn't know that person at all.

I DON'T BELIEVE in God. Not right now. Not at this minute. But . . .

When they cut Nick Gorden down from the upper stairwell outside the chem lab, a storm had just come up over the lake. You know the kind: lightning, rain, and wind that rips the roofs off buildings.

Ohio isn't Tornado Alley, but it comes pretty damn close. I hate it here in the spring and summer. I've just always wanted to be somewhere that nature couldn't rip my head off, and always said so. That used to make Nick laugh, 'cause he said you couldn't hide from weather— it was everywhere.

They were gentle when they took Nick away. The paramedics put him on the stretcher like he was a baby. I didn't see the rest, the cops and all. I only watched through a second-floor window as they took my best friend away from me and here and this place—forever . . .

I tell Chris (she wants to be called Chris), the therapist, that there had to be a storm the day Nick died. Something cataclysmic and ugly had to happen. If the sun had been shining, afterward maybe I would have cried and thought about how Nick just missed a happening day at the park or hangin' around Doggy's Cafe eating cheese jalapeno onion dogs. But as it happened, nature stepped in again. Somebody had to cry for Nick.

The sky and his mother did that day.

My eyes stayed dry.

I've learned that you can't ask for too much, even though I never ask at all.

I've always sort of taken what was hangin' around or skulked around for leftovers.

Chris says that's too bad. (Yeah.) So she writes down a few words on a piece of paper and hands it to me before I leave her office and head for the Rapid. I read it as the train shoots me back into the suburbs.

It says:

ASK FOR TWO THINGS YOU'VE ALWAYS WANTED, BUT NEVER THOUGHT TO REQUEST

I think of one thing I'd ask for now that I never had to ask for before. Then some man gets on the train with five hundred bags and two jelly-faced kids, and they sit right beside me. I forget about everything as I ride back into the burbs.

It's all about Nick. All of it.

The therapy, the dreams, the way I can't cry . . .

Nick's favorite song was an old Sly & the Family Stone tune called "Everybody Is a Star." He sang it all the time. Wrote and tagged buildings everywhere with it, but in the end he didn't believe it, I guess.

It was the song Nick's uncle was singing right before he died in Vietnam. Nick's mom got all her brother's belongings—clothes, records, dog tags—from one of the guys in his platoon. That was better than some stranger showing up handing her the stuff.

Nick played his uncle's records.

No CD or even cassettes ever came into the house (Nick and his mom seemed satisfied with their records). So Nick used to go to Spin-More downtown to find 45s and albums.

It used to drive me crazy listening to those old records with scratches and jumps in them, but Nick said the scratches were in his head—he knew every one of them and they were like old friends. CDs were cold and if one messed up, you couldn't put a penny on the arm of a CD to weight it down so that it wouldn't jump.

I never told Nick those records bothered me. Now I wish I had, 'cause at least it would have been one more conversation we had had.

You never understand some things until the end. Hindsight. Some things you may never understand at all.

I used to be envious of Nick, 'cause he was the person that everybody said hello to in the halls. He always smiled and seemed to sail along halls that had nothing but fear in them (to me, at least). In class pictures he always smiled. In his family pictures he always smiled.

I overheard his mom on the phone once call him sweet and good-natured.

But I found out something about Nick a week before he died that got me all turned around, and I'd known Nick since first grade. We had been each other's one and only friend since he'd followed me under the monkey bars after I'd stolen Josh Neil's lunch (Josh had hit me with an eraser earlier).

Nick had crawled under and sat beside me while I munched. He stared at me until I gave him a Fruit Roll-Up to go away. He ate it, kept staring, and stayed.

The next day the same thing, only this time I'd taken pudding out of Heather Longchamp's backpack 'cause she'd sat on me in front of the whole first grade. Plus she always had butterscotch.

We finally got caught a week later. My mom dragged me out of the office mumbling that I was already a criminal.

Nick told the principal *he'd* taken the lunches and I said *I'd* taken them. I couldn't go out and play for two weeks. Nick's mom bought him butterscotch pudding for his lunch.

Okay, we were tight; so why didn't I understand that even though Nick was somebody people smiled at and waved to, nobody knew anything about him? Sometimes they couldn't even remember his name. Nick said it. He was the invisible man.

The week before they took him out on a stretcher with his face covered, Mr. Miles (in civics class) couldn't remember his name or that he had even been in the class. I think Nick could have taken that if Heather (no longer eating pudding—a definite anorexic) hadn't started laughing that he'd been going to school for years and nobody ever knew his name.

I wanted to hit her. Break those skinny, skinny cheerleader arms and that big-toothed smile she only used to torture people.

Everybody laughed but me and Mr. Miles, who just looked confused and a little sorry he'd opened his mouth. Nick was even laughing.

I spent the rest of the day with a stomachache, not able to look Nick in the eye. Later that night he laughed that invisible people had to have a sense of humor. I didn't think that was funny.

I wasn't invisible myself. I was just visible enough to be left out of conversations purposefully—just visible enough to be picked on for my bad skin, nonexistent fashion sense, and the biggest crime of all: I was smarter than anyone in my class and I had the nerve to be female.

That night Nick stood on his bed, stared at his poster of Dennis Rodman, and said, "Bow to those who rage on."

I went over to Nick's house after the police and all the social workers and neighbors had gone back to their lives.

At first I was going to knock on the door, but then I couldn't face Miss Gorden. Her eyes would be puffy, her face tired and sad, her body drooping. I climbed into the open hall window on the side of the house. It's the way me and Nick came in most of the time anyway.

I could hear Miss Gorden crying two rooms down. She sounded like a little kid. I almost started crying too. That would have been a good thing. That would have helped. Everybody says so. But instead I just ducked into Nick's room.

His basketball and Greenpeace posters jumped out at me and stabbed me in the heart. I used to listen to guys at school talking basketball as Nick's eyes glowed. I'd think: This time he's going to say something, talk about what happened in some game somewhere. But he never did, and none of the group ever asked.

I curled up on the bed and looked around the room. It was a friendly mess. It sat there waiting for Nick to come back to it. Maybe dream and imagine in it. I closed my eyes and in a minute was asleep.

When I woke up a few hours later, the sun was going down and Miss Gorden must have come in and taken Nick's favorite blanket off his chair and covered me in it. I pulled it over my head and inhaled Nick, then crawled out the way I came in and walked the street-lit sidewalks.

Nick's mom wanted me to pick out what he'd be buried in. I guess she knew she'd feel compelled to pick out a suit. Neither of us wanted to think about Nick in a suit forever. Of course I say forever, 'cause I don't believe in God or anything after this. And forever is a damn long time.

I chose his favorite khakis and his Greenpeace sweatshirt. I hopped a bus and took it to the funeral home, where everybody whispered at me and was nice.

I got back on the bus and watched the world pass by, with the paper sack that I had carried Nick's clothes in still in my hand.

At breakfast yesterday my dad said, "Do you want to go to another school?"

I bit down hard on my apple without looking at him, then slurped my orange juice so that I couldn't hear him if he asked the question again.

He asked again.

So I grabbed a piece of toast and hoped it was as loud as the apple had been.

"Nia, did you hear me?"

I had.

He shook his head and looked at my mom, who was looking again for signs that I was so depressed I'd go the way Nick had. Finally, though, they started picking up the breakfast dishes and left me alone.

I'd have to get used to alone.

I stood beside Miss Gorden when they put her son in the ground. I fought the urge to scream when the casket was lowered. I should have screamed.

There were eight people there: Miss Gorden, my parents and me, the school principal, and three people I'd never seen before.

Again I wanted to scream. Nobody from school came. Not one classmate. Not even to get out of those halls from hell.

Everyone cried but me.

When the service ended, Miss Gorden turned on the boom box she'd told me to bring. She sat it next to

Nick's grave and smiled as "Everybody Is a Star" echoed through the cemetery. And all I could think as I got into my mom's minivan was that Nick probably wouldn't even be mad that the last time he heard his song it was on a CD.

For a week the halls and classes got quiet when I walked through them. It was like carrying a plague that would only infect others if they talked around you. They all just stayed away. I'd never gotten so much attention in my whole life by being ignored.

The second week, though, it started. The questions.

Why? And why *there?*

Did I expect it?

Did he talk about it?

I would swallow what I wanted to say and never answer.

Did they fuckin' want me to put in a paragraph or less (while looking appropriately sad) how someone I loved more than anyone on the planet had lived his life, then ended it? Especially to people who couldn't give a damn whether he lived or died before he died.

Had most of the apple-smelling, Gap-wearing pack creatures ever held a single conversation with Nick?

Had any of the ones who ask me "How come?" been in a group who had screamed out "Do it!" as Nick was about to let go of the rafters and swing like a rag doll in front of them?

I lasted three days in school.

I wrote "NICK WAS HAPPY" 3,549 times on my Grrlll Power notebook.

Then—

Nick had been happy his whole life. He'd never had a bad day his whole life, I thought. He never seemed miserable or lonely, 'cause he had me. I thought he never minded that he was invisible. I'd always believed he never wanted to be like them, having basketball conversations and talking about what they did the night before. I guess I was wrong about it all.

Wrong that he never minded that they thought he was a sad case 'cause his best friend was a girl with bad skin who couldn't form a social sentence. Wrong that it didn't make him sad that the person he identified with most was a boy who'd died thirteen years before he was born, fighting a war that never should have been. At thirteen when Nick found out about reincarnation, he decided his uncle had come back to the world as him.

He really believed it. Believed it in his soul. Believed it more than anything he'd ever thought in his whole life, even believed it more than the thing about him being invisible.

Heather Longchamp sees me at the Dairy Mart and tosses her sweet-smelling, shining hair off her shoulders before she says quietly, "I'm so sorry about your friend . . . Ummm—"

"Nick," I say, trying to act like I've dropped change on the floor, but only looking like somebody losing her mind (which I already have).

"Yeah, yeah, Nick," she says before she spots somebody she has to talk to outside in a brand-new black SUV.

I walk out of the Dairy Mart in a trance, then throw up all over the parking lot.

I watch the world through a window of Sarah Elizabeth Hollcomb Psychiatric Clinic for Adolescents, and the world only comes in and bothers me when I want it to.

I've decided that it's not such a bad thing to be invisible. The thing that you have to be careful of, the thing that Nick never learned, is that you can't want to be anything else. You can't want to have more people who care.

You have to be invisible on your own all by yourself. You can't even have a friend like me who loves you and thinks you're better than anything else.

Nick got it wrong. Everybody isn't a star. Shit, maybe in a better world they could be.

They could be. They really could be.

Amen.

Angela Johnson

From her very first publication, reviewers recognized Angela Johnson as a promising writer for young people. Her picture book *When I Am Old with You*, with illustrations by David Soman, received the PEN/Norma Klein Award, the Ezra Jack Keats New Writer Award, and a Coretta Scott King Honor. Since then Angela Johnson has published more than a dozen picture books, four novels for teenagers, a book of poems, most of which have also won prestigious awards, and a collection of short stories titled *Gone from Home: Short Takes.*

Toning the Sweep, her first young adult novel, won the 1994 Coretta Scott King Award, as well as being named a *School Library Journal* Best Book, an American Library Association Best Book for Young Adults, and a *Booklist* Editors' Choice. *Humming Whispers* was an ALA Quick Pick selection; *Songs of Faith* was an *American Bookseller* Pick of the Lists; *The Other Side: Shorter Poems* was a Coretta Scott King Honor Book as well as a Lee Bennett Hopkins Poetry Award winner. And in 1999 *Heaven* received the Coretta Scott King Award and was named a Best Book for Young Adults by the ALA.

In all of Angela Johnson's works, family relationships and communication are important themes, as they are in her story "Through a Window." She says she had two objects in mind when she wrote this story: "to ask the unanswerable questions that float around when a seemingly content young person takes their life," and to examine "what happens to a friend left behind . . . who was unable to do anything about it. I was interested in writing about a nonviolent, basically nonharassed teen, unseen by most of his peers, and the consequences that may result from being unseen."

Muzak for Prozac

Jack Gantos

*He's cool, relaxed, composed. Soothing music and drug
therapy keep him feeling mellow, in control. Without them
he will never reach his goal, never be able to tell her . . .
Can he do it today?*

EVERYONE HAS HIS own Prozac ritual. Here is mine. At
exactly 10:00 A.M., before I leave the house for my des-
tination, I boil water and pour it into a small chrome
thermos. I always place the capsule of Prozac in my left
side shirt pocket. Then I get into my blue Metro and
drive the exact speed limit, which usually means
everyone passes me by. I never pass anyone. Never. I'm
good to go—fast or slow. If you do five miles an hour,
I'm right behind you at five miles an hour, big smile on
my face, tape player headphones clamped down on my
noggin, both hands on the wheel. I'm not muttering,
cursing, giving you the bird, or reaching into the glove

compartment for my plastic Glock 9mm. None of that confrontational behavior for me. I've got time to kill.

When I finally make it to the Publix supermarket I always park far away from the front door, usually in the farthest back row where all the employees park. The girl I've come to see is a cashier here, and this is where she leaves her silver Toyota Corolla.

I always back into my space so that later, when I'm a bit rattled from trying to speak with her, I can just pull smoothly straight out and putt-putt away like a good boy. Once I park my car and turn off the engine I open my thermos and pour a cupful of hot water into the screw cap top. I hold it just beneath my nose and sniff it. One whiff and I can tell how hot it is. I like to blow softly over the cup and allow the rising steam to fog my glasses. Then I stare out across the parking lot, and the flurry of shapes are just smudges of color, as if I'm staring out at a reef of odd fish. I close my eyes. I turn up the Mystic Moods Orchestra on my tape player and meditate on the single circling note of a French horn as it disembarks into the blissful wilderness of shimmering triangles. The music is important. It has to be seamless. No jagged edges. Just a cocoon of silken notes in suspended animation. The Mystic Moods Orchestra is the best for this kind of reverie. I highly recommend them.

Then I wipe the fingers of my right hand across the leg of my jeans and reach into my shirt pocket. I pluck out the green-and-white Prozac capsule, place it like a cat's eye on the tip of my tongue, and as I roll my tongue into my mouth I follow it with a flush of warm water. And when I swallow I feel the Prozac cascading down my throat like a life preserver over Niagara Falls.

"Here I come," the Prozac says to me in a clinician's sexy voice. "Wash those troubles away and get ready to say yes to everything."

I smile. I love saying yes to everything.

It doesn't take long. The hot water speeds up the process. The marvelous quality of Prozac is that you don't get high. You just get an extremely serene feeling because the Prozac floats you down the path of least resistance where you constantly make all the correct decisions. You don't sense a tangible change in how you think, or feel, or move your body. What you feel is clean, nimble. Normal. I'm not talking high or not high—like Valium or Librium. Those inferior drugs wilted the anxiety in me so that all day I was flopped over the sofa like one of Dalí's drowsy clocks. Not Prozac. It does nothing to you physically. The secret in the formula is that it allows you the supreme pleasure to love everything you do. Not in a giddy way. Not like breathing laughing gas. Or smoking dope and getting the giggles. Nothing so juvenile. No, Prozac allows you to give up resisting. It keeps you from dwelling on what you should have done, should have said, should have accomplished, should have handled, and gives you the smooth advantage of accepting everything you do as well done. It lets you think and feel everything at the *exact* moment you do and think and feel it. There is no delay in the satisfaction achieved. It is immediate. It is yours. It takes the sting out of life. You become good. Right. Fulfilled. This is Prozac. "Yes," it says, "please help yourself. Enjoy."

"Thank you," I reply. "Don't mind if I do."

As I approach the grocery store I begin to hum, "Row,

row, row your boat gently down the stream. Merrily, merrily, merrily, merrily, life is but a dream." When you time the ingestion and infusion of the Prozac just right it's as if you are in your own movie where every detail has been precisely thought out, every step and gesture choreographed, each word scripted, and you are the star. Just when I expect my celebrity photograph to be taken I trip the eye of the automatic door, and it opens its wide arms to give me the red carpet treatment. I step across the threshold, wipe my feet, and feel so welcome, so fresh—as if I've just stepped out of the tub into a plush, heated bathroom, skin all warm and moist and pink and slightly puckered in the amniotic steam. Every pore, every hair and little crease of flesh all as sparkling clean as something manufactured. Flawless. Happy. When I get that angelic Prozac lift, I just gaze into the eyes of the first person I see, and with a suede whisper I say, "Have a nice day," as if I'm a bright yellow smiley face come alive.

I'm so, so happy as I adjust the volume of Brian Eno's "Ambient 4" to wall out the store music, which is just a set of easy-listening Motown classics for the mom-and-baby duos to sing along with. One thing about Prozac, it does not like lyrics butting in, banging at the door of gentle consciousness. No, Prozac is sound without meaning. Lyrics have such a negative impact. Just hearing them is like being bullied around, like twitching over and over to a skip in a record. Really annoying. I go for the pure 101 Strings just lifting the swollen spirit above all the bad memories inside me that are trying to bring me down. Because when I feel myself being tugged at again by the bad things I did, my reflex response is that

I've got to resist, I've got to fight back, take a stand. And then my whole comfortable pillow is ruined. My cushion is blown and I have to be alert, vigilant, ever paranoid, self-serving, tough, determined, driven, and above all, a survivor.

Not me. I'm doomed to orchestral easy listening, which is a cleansing bleach to all that inner hubbub.

The first action I take in the grocery store is to grab a cart and dash over to the fruit and vegetable section where I know she can't see me from her position at the number eleven checkout aisle. I try not to look her way but I find it impossible. I spot her red hair right off, and then I slam directly into a table of lemons. If I was designing shopping carts, they would be like big marshmallows on air-cushioned wheels so that if you banged into a corner you wouldn't hear a sound like a tray of silverware dropping on the floor. No. My carts would have crumple zones, maybe even bumpers that release a few bars of the Sandpipers doing "Softly." But not a crash.

Which brings me to food color. You take a good look at pastels and, really, your spirits soar like Peter Nero on a Love Trip. I could stare at the color of a slightly ripe apricot for hours. It's dreamy. The color says, Settle down. Stay calm. Eat me. I love you. I forgive you. And then look at an artichoke. That shade of green is the color of bile. And the outer thorn-tipped petals are always scarred from defending themselves against being tossed around, handled roughly, pitched into bushel bins by callused hands. They've been treated with bad intentions. And they just bring it on themselves from being so eager to hurt you all the time. So they get boiled, or just left to rot.

And lettuce. What I like is when they mist the coolers and the vegetables are covered in evenly spaced droplets of water, as if sewn on like sequins. Once, I pressed my face so close to the verdant green leaves of the romaine that I couldn't see anything more than rolling hills of emerald, and I timed a deep breath with the upbeat of Kostelanetz's magic wand of harmony and was transported into a world so Jurassic it was infinitely moist. I don't know how long I stood there and meditated on that chord of perfection but it wasn't until the misting machine came back on that the spray of water brought me around to the present moment.

That was deep.

Today the lemons are a study in yellow. And yellow, as any artist will tell you, is the most unstable color in the palate. Too much red and it turns to orange like that self-tanning lotion. Too much white and it becomes pale, dingy really, like cheap linoleum that's worn. Ugly. But when I stare into that cascade of lemons I think only one word: "Lemon." And I feel as though I'm filled with lemon cream inside, like a ladyfinger. And there is only one perfect lemon serenade: "Happy Heart" by Roger Williams. I put a few in my cart, then push on. I have things to do.

One of my first jobs is to calm down the angry toy aisle with those little soldiers and guns and plastic swords and Star Wars Blasters that wait for me like a gauntlet of bullies. But I melt them, diffuse them. Ionize them and turn them into pacifists with a dose of Hi-Fi Zither. After that you can just feel those toys wanting to flee their bad intentions, leaving their plastic atoms begging for a meltdown into a mold of beach balls and hula hoops.

When I get to the end of the aisle I stand there and watch her checking out a lady's groceries. She is concentrating fully on her task of rotating each item so that the binary code is facedown to the scanner. I am so close I can hear the tiny beeps as the cash register records the prices. If I could just move forward about twenty feet I would be queued up in her line, and then I could say "I'm sorry." That's all. That's all my therapist says I have to say. "Sorry." And if I went through her checkout line I could say sorry just as casually as everyone else says "Have a nice day."

But I'm just not ready to move twenty feet forward. Not yet. I'm not in the right mood to face her, so I glide away to the right. I feel a strong need for totally supportive food in my cart. Smiling bananas. Loaves of fresh, soft bread. Butter. No cans. Nothing spicy. Rice is good. I love how when you try to count the grains in a see-through bag of rice it might be an hour or so before you can pull your gaze away while saying, "Three thousand five hundred and ninety-nine." Cool Whip is good. Baby custard. Very ripe fruit. A twelve-pack of extra-soft bathroom tissue.

Many times I've tried to say I'm sorry to her. And failed. Once I never made it into the store. I just stayed out in the parking lot and when people finished loading their groceries into their cars I returned their carts. I kept the parking lot tidied up and after a couple of hours a kid in a green apron came out of the store and asked me if I wanted a job and I said no, it was time to go home now.

About a week later I returned to the store ready to try again to say I was sorry. I made it through the front door but I got sidetracked at the lobster tank. They were so sad. They needed me. I took all the rubber bands off their claws and they got into a big clenched up ball and I was asked to leave the store. Nicely, but firmly, I marched to the exit. No one had to touch me.

Then about a week ago I was doing a little shopping and listening to a compilation tape of twelve Mood Masters doing "Tiptoe Through the Tulips," and I got so giddy I opened up all the potato chip bags and covered the entire aisle. That field of crunchy golden chips was as serene to me as tulips were to Tiny Tim. I never had the chance to say sorry that day either.

I know what you're thinking. That I'm a loser. But I promise, today will be different. I feel totally centered. I feel I'll regain my pride. I'll look her in the eye and say sorry and move on. I'll be better for it. A goal met, and a cure realized. And to further prepare me for success, there is a massage demonstration at the natural foods and organic products kiosk. It's my lucky day.

"Would you like a free fifteen-minute massage?" the woman says as I stop my cart. "It will increase your energy." She is wearing a white turban. In fact, she is all in white, like a Sufi nurse, and she is so pure and her skin is microscopically clean. Her teeth are good.

"Yes," I reply. "This is just what I need." I climb into the special chair that cradles me forward and I rest my face in a cushioned oval so that I feel a bit weightless.

She removes my headphones and puts her own on me. It is a NatureQuest tape of a waterfall, and I immediately give in to the seductive sameness of it. Very soothing.

She starts with my neck. Gently. And the more I relax the more my mind goes blank. Black, with specks of nervous color. And I like it that way, as if I'm in a movie theater staring up at a dark screen. But it doesn't stay that way. Each time her thumbs knead the base of my neck it's as if she is a magician summoning up what I want to hide.

Then the feature show begins.

It was a needy period in my life. I wanted people to like me for who I was. But I had nothing to offer. So I offered them something else. The checkout girl. I outed her. I was walking on the golf course at night to escape the city lights. I had my telescope and book of star charts. The moon was full and the grass stood up like silver spikes. The shadows from the swaying trees opened and closed like stage curtains. I was walking up the fairway, listening to the synthetic Harmony Makers, when I suddenly saw her—the girl from my school, the checkout girl. She was with another girl, someone I had passed in the halls. They had a blanket spread out on the eighth green. Quickly, I retreated into the pines beyond the rough. I set up my telescope. They kissed. They had sex. I saw it all. And then, like a village idiot, I couldn't keep my mouth shut. The next day I told everything I saw to everyone I knew, or hardly knew, and before long I had my fifteen minutes of fame. It seemed that the entire school lined up to hear what I had to say. After that, the fame turned to regret as I witnessed how people turned against them.

It wasn't nice, but it wasn't especially sinister. The other students' meanness was just plain vanilla meanness. Or so I thought. I wasn't the one who was being treated like a freak, so it was hard for me to tell. Then there was the suicide attempt. They took pills. One died and the other didn't. I sure wish they hadn't done that because it made me feel very bad. The survivor was sent away to a mental institution. I thought I'd never see her again, which was a relief. But I wasn't off the hook. She returned. Not to our school, but to our town. By accident I ran into her at the grocery store. She was working as a checkout girl. I started to go through her line, then she took one long look at me and all the shame inside me let loose. She knew I was her Judas and I hated myself and like Judas I thought I would explode, thought my knotted guts would burst out and I would die an agonizing death. So I backed out of the line. I left my cart of food and ran out of the store. Ran like the loser Judas I was and went home to my room and stayed there.

After a while my parents took me to a therapist. I adore my therapist. She has a way of making every word come out of her mouth as round as a smoke ring. Even though we've gone over and over the fact that I didn't anticipate what my actions would set off—that it was their choice to take the pills—it had still been my choice to turn them in for my little bit of popularity. So, because I couldn't talk my way out of my shame, I began to take the medication. The Prozac. It has helped. I no longer feel dangerous to myself. I say yes to just about everything I think. I figure since there is no resistance, there is no growth. But I'm not in pursuit of personal growth. I'm just looking to keep calm. I don't want to hurt myself.

Suddenly the Sufi nurse cracks my back and I have no idea where I am and I can't tell whether if I'm sitting right-side up or upside down.

"Stop!" I shout. "Stop!"

"But I'm not finished," she says.

"I am," I say, and wrestle myself out of the chair. "Thanks," I say, blinking. Then I hold on to my cart and shove off.

I need to calm down. I turn right, down the ice cream aisle. It is quiet and cool. I put on my Philip Glass and his frenetic rhythms get me going on a fresh idea. There is nothing wrong with moving quickly. With both hands I begin to remove half-gallon boxes of ice cream from the tall coolers. Vanilla, Chocolate, Strawberry, Neapolitan. I love them all, and as I stack them up I begin to lay the circular foundation for an igloo. My hands are cold, numb really, but it excites me to touch something and *feel* nothing. A woman starts down my aisle, then abruptly turns around. I work faster and faster. I get the second course up, shifting it toward the center like the ceiling of the Pantheon. I empty the first freezer compartment. I look down the aisle. Still no manager. So I begin on the next freezer. I soon have the third course down. All Rum Raisin. Then a fourth of Mocha Crunch. My concentration is spot-on and before long I have the walls of the igloo up to my hips, and then I panic. I get a taste of something like vinegar in my mouth—something sharp and salty—and I just stand there. It's wearing off. The Prozac is being pulled away like a magnet pulling away metal shavings. I open my hand and sniff the palm. I'm sweating and I smell bad.

Then in a moment of genius I write SORRY on the fogged-over freezer doors. SORRY, SORRY, SORRY, all the way down the aisle.

When I finish I'm smiling. My day is not a failure. I got a little closer to completing my mission. Tomorrow I'm sure I'll face up to her. Maybe buy a little ice cream and ask if she'd like to share it with me. But now it's time to go. A manager has just pointed his finger at me.

Jack Gantos

Younger readers know Jack Gantos as the creator of Rotten Ralph, the award-winning picture book series. Most recently, Rotten Ralph has been developed into an animated series by the BBC and Fox.

For middle-school readers, Jack Gantos has retold adventures from his own wacky youth in a series of hilarious novels about Jack Henry: *Heads or Tails: Stories from the Sixth Grade*, *Jack's New Power: Stories from a Caribbean Year*, *Jack's Black Book*, and *Jack on the Tracks: Four Seasons of Fifth Grade*.

The funny business continues in Gantos's *Joey Pigsa Swallowed the Key*, which was a National Book Award finalist. Readers who laughed out loud at Joey's antics in that book will want to see what else happens to him in *Joey Pigsa Loses Control*.

In his young adult novel, *Desire Lines*, Gantos leaves his oddball humor behind to look at what happens when a young man exposes the secret relationship between two girls in his high school. That romance and the double suicide attempt that follow its exposure were based on a real event. One of the girls had been Jack's high school lab partner. Although he had not been the one who exposed the relationship between the two girls, he says, "I've always felt guilty for not providing what small emotional support I could. Months after the incident, when I saw her working in a nearby town, I had a great urge to tell her how sorry I was that her friend had died. But I didn't raise the courage to do so." "Muzak for Prozac" is another outgrowth of those guilty feelings, with the main character being "one pathetic manifestation of my cowardice," he says.

Standing on the Roof Naked

Francess Lantz

*Jeannie feels different from everyone else in her school.
Looks different too: She's skinny and flat-chested and prefers
to dress like a boy. Some of the boys don't like that. But
what can she do about it?*

SUPPOSEDLY, THERE AREN'T any tomboys anymore.
No need. Nowadays, girls can be anything we want to
be. Astronauts, construction workers, basketball stars.
Why would any self-respecting girl want to act like a
guy? We can be female and still do it all.

So then why did the Spice Girls, those so-called
spokeswomen of Girl Power, wear miniskirts up to their
pubic hair? Why do the girls in my school giggle and
preen whenever a cute guy walks by? And why is it
most of the girls I know spend more money on a single
haircut than the average Ethiopian family spends on
food for an entire year?

Believe me, feminism is a long, long way from becoming a reality. So don't blame me if I don't want to dress like a stripper and act dumb just to make some loser stud feel important. I'm no hypocrite. I'm walking the walk, not just talking the talk.

Only the truth is, that's just the story I tell myself to feel better. Actually, I don't know why I wanted to be a boy until I was thirteen years old, and why, to this day, I still feel more comfortable in baggy boy clothes than dresses. Or why my hair is short and tangled and in my eyes instead of long and silky like some Pantene commercial. And I can't explain why I'd rather stay home and listen to CDs than go to a school dance. Or why, at fifteen, I still haven't even kissed a boy, let alone done the dirty deed. All I know is that I'm different. And in this world, let me tell you, different is not good.

It's Monday morning and I'm at school. Walking alone, as usual. I used to have friends, back in middle school when there were still girls who hadn't grown breasts and most of the boys were shorter than us and smelled like a hamper of damp sweat socks. Nan, Chrissy, and I spent our days climbing trees, making crank phone calls, and writing in our secret spy journals. Life was good.

Then Chrissy's parents got divorced and she moved to the New Jersey shore with her mom, and Nan got her period and started going steady with Brad Hafner. Suddenly, I was alone. Suddenly, I was different. And no one was going to let me forget it.

"Hey, Johnny," Rory Peterson calls as I walk past.

Actually, my name is Jeannie, but the jocks who like to harass me think it's a hoot to call me John.

"Nothin' wrong with her that a hot date wouldn't cure," Mike Forelli says.

"Yeah, right—a hot date with a hot dyke," Rory snickers.

Suzanne Mendoza walks up to Rory. They've been dating most of the year. "Leave her alone," she says. "She's harmless."

Suzanne Mendoza is the star of the girls' soccer team. She's twice as big as me, with broad shoulders and muscular legs, but no one calls *her* a dyke. That's because she's got big boobs and goes out with Rory.

Too bad I'm skinny and flat-chested and suck at sports. But it's not too bad that I'm not going out with Rory. I'd rather kiss a maggot-ridden dog than feel Rory's hands on my body.

But whose hands do I want to feel? I don't know.

"Hey, Johnny," Mike taunts, "why don't you ask Suzanne out for a date? I'll bet she's just your type."

"Mike!" Suzanne scolds. She shoves him, and Mike and Rory snicker. I picture myself blowing the three of them away with a bazooka. Or maybe I'd rather invite them to a tea party and slip strychnine in their scones. How's that for ladylike behavior?

But what I actually do is lower my head and walk on.

At home Mom greets me at the door with a smile and a plate of peanut butter cookies. She's a beautiful woman, always nicely dressed, every auburn hair in place. I don't think I've ever seen her without makeup.

"How was your day?" she asks.

"Okay." I take a cookie and toss my backpack on the sofa.

"The doctor came by today."

I freeze. The cookie feels like it's coming up in my throat.

"Daddy ate a little more today. Dr. Heidleman was pleased."

I let out a breath and will my shoulders to relax. My father hasn't been taken to the hospital. He isn't dead.

I watch my mother as she puts the plate of cookies on the coffee table. She's so graceful, so controlled. When she was a little girl, she wanted to be a ballet dancer. She took lessons for years, but gave it up in college when she met Dad.

I want to ask her what's wrong with my father, but I can't. I don't want to know. Or maybe it's that I really do know. He's got cancer. But Mom never uses the C word. "He's under the weather," she says. Or, "He's feeling poorly."

He's dying! I want to scream. Only I don't. I reach for another cookie and scarf it down.

"You're getting crumbs on the sofa," Mom frets.

I should go in and see him. He's in the spare bedroom, which Mom turned into an office for him when he couldn't go to work anymore. Only he never used it. He went in there, skimmed through a couple of law books, and lay down on the bed. That was three weeks ago and he's still in there. Mostly, he just sleeps.

"I've got a lot of homework," I say.

I get up and go into the hall. I pause by the spare bedroom, but I'm frightened to look inside. What will he look like? What will he say? Will he even recognize me?

I hurry into my room and close the door.

* * *

I was four years old when I first announced that I wanted to be a boy. "No you don't," my mother said. So, to prove I meant what I said, I sawed the head off my Barbie doll and baked it in my Betty Crocker oven.

Mom responded by buying me a new dress. "Try it on," she urged. "It will look so pretty with your blue eyes."

I put on the dress, then went outside and climbed the cherry tree. When I came in for lunch the dress was ripped and smudged and covered with cherry juice.

Mom was upset—I could see it in her eyes—but she didn't get mad. She never does. I try to be like her, but it's hard. I'm mad all the time—at Rory Peterson and his brain-dead buddies, at my father for getting sick, at myself for being such a freak.

At lunch on Fridays we're allowed to play CDs in the cafeteria. Different kids take turns acting as DJ. The popular kids get up and dance.

Today I come into the cafeteria and see a kid setting up a couple of turntables. I've seen him around before, but I don't know his name. He's over six feet tall and skinny, with pale skin and spiky black hair. He reminds me of a spider, but not a dangerous one. A daddy longlegs maybe.

He sets up a microphone and starts to spin a stack of record albums. He's spinning and scratching, switching from record to record. It's all old soul music, really funky stuff like James Brown and Parliament/Funkadelic. Sometimes he turns to the CD player and pops in a current tune, then lays down a beat behind it on the turntable.

I look around to see how the school is reacting. No one is dancing. Everyone is just staring at this kid. I'm staring too. He's really putting on a show. I notice a few jocks are whispering and snickering. They can't deal with anything new or different. Their motto is: If it's unusual, it must be ridiculed.

But lots of other kids are bobbing their heads along with the beat. It's irresistible. I'm doing it too.

Who is this dude? When the bell rings, I walk past the turntables. "Hey, Reilly," someone calls. He looks up.

Now I know his name.

Last week I saw a book in Borders called *Lesbian Couples*. Some of the women in it looked like me—skinny and flat-chested, with short hair and no makeup.

Is that what I am? I wonder. A lesbian?

I try to imagine kissing a girl. Strange. I try to imagine kissing a boy. Also strange.

What's wrong with me?

When I was six, I started drawing pictures of car wrecks and plane crashes. Lots of blood, lots of severed body parts. My parents were in shock.

"You've never seen a serious accident," my mother said, eyeing my latest drawing, a gory train wreck. "And I pray to God you never will. Why would you want to draw such a thing?"

"I like it."

I couldn't explain it any better than that. All I knew was that when I drew those pictures, I felt wild, I felt free. Like standing on the roof naked, screaming my lungs out.

Now it's music that does that for me. Nine Inch Nails blasting through the house when my parents aren't home, making the walls tremble, making *me* tremble.

Or watching Reilly lay down those beats at lunch the other day. I wish I had the talent to get up in front of everybody and do that. I wish I had the nerve.

I see an ad in the arts section of the Sunday paper for a bookstore/cafe in Philadelphia called Brand New Day. FULL SELECTION OF LESBIAN BOOKS, CASSETTES, AND CDS, the ad says. LIVE MUSIC ON SATURDAY NIGHTS. THIS SATURDAY: BELLADONNA.

On Saturday afternoon, I take the train into the city. The bookstore is on South Street. I stand outside for a long time, getting up the courage to go in.

Finally, my numb fingers and tingling nose force me inside. The woman behind the cash register looks up and smiles. Can she read in my eyes what I am? Lesbian? Or impostor? I wish she'd tell me.

I wander the aisles, looking at the books. Did you know there are lesbian travel guides? Lesbian self-help books? Lesbian porno? I hide behind a greeting card rack and open a short story collection called *Encounters*. Whoa! I've never read anything like that before, straight *or* gay.

I stay so long, the band is into their sound check. The lights are being lowered and the venetian blinds on the windows are being drawn. The tables and chairs in the cafe section are filled, mostly with women in their twenties and thirties. I stare at them, trying to recognize myself in their faces. But they all look so comfortable in their bodies, so relaxed and self-assured, I feel like a stranger.

Then the music starts. There's a piano player, bass and drums, a singer. They're playing jazz and some up-tempo swing tunes. A few women get up and dance. Arms around each other, cheek against cheek. I try not to stare, but I can't help it.

"Would you like to dance?"

I look up to see a woman in her early twenties, with red hair and brown eyes. Oh, my God, she's talking to me!

"I—I don't know how," I sputter, stepping backward.

"I'll teach you."

She takes my hand and leads me onto the floor. My heart is pounding, pits flooding. Her arms are around me now, and she's trying to show me some dance step. I hear her voice, but I can't make sense of the words. All I know is the feel of her palm on my spine, her hip pressed against my hip.

I break away, frightened and embarrassed, and mutter something about the bathroom. I'm stumbling through a sea of undulating bodies, searching for the door, then plunging headlong into the frigid night.

It didn't feel right, I know that. But would it have been any different with a guy? Maybe it's just me. I don't know how to touch people, how to look another human being in the eye. My head has been down too long, following my shuffling feet.

Mom has started sleeping in the La-Z-Boy recliner in the spare bedroom. That must mean my father is getting worse. I peeked in at him yesterday morning. His cheeks were covered with stubble and his hair was mussed. And his body under the covers, it looked so small, more like a child's than a man's. He didn't see me. He was staring at the wall, at nothing.

Nighttime. I lie balled up in the corner of my bed, listening. Each time my mother gets up out of the La-Z-Boy, I hold my breath. If I can hold it until she sits back down, my father won't die.

Now she walks into the hallway. I can hear her footsteps coming my way. My stomach clenches. She's coming to tell me he's dead, he's dead, he's dead.

She turns off into the bathroom and shuts the door. I allow myself to breathe, but my stomach won't unclench. I wrap my arms around my legs and go on waiting.

"Jeannie, do you know Reilly Briggs?" Mrs. Filbert asks. "He's the boy who was playing records in the cafeteria last week."

"Not really."

"He's in my third-period class. He told me he's looking for someone to write raps to his beats. I thought of you."

"I don't know how to rap," I protest.

"You've written some good poems this year. I'm sure you could write a rap."

Yeah, right. My poems are just free-form thoughts. They don't even rhyme. Shows how much Mrs. Filbert knows about rap music.

"I gave him your name," she says. "I hope that's all right."

My cheeks are burning. I feel like simultaneously doing a cartwheel and dropping out of school immediately. Then I realize Reilly probably won't take the trouble to seek me out. He undoubtedly thinks Mrs. Filbert is as lame as I do. Anyone she suggests would have to be a complete loser.

I briefly consider approaching him, then quickly change my mind. What would I say? In any case, I can't write a rap, don't even want to. So why bother?

I feel relieved. And disappointed.

It's study hall and I get a pass to go to the restroom. Oh, shit. Rory Petersen and Mike Forelli are hanging out in the hall near the water fountain. I do an about-face, but it's too late. They see me.

"Hey, Johnny, need to use the boys' room?" Rory calls, coming in close to leer at me.

Mike sidles up behind me, cutting off my path of escape. "Do you think she pees standing up?" he muses.

"Maybe *she* is actually a *he*," Rory announces. "I mean, what if old Johnny isn't a girl who wants to be a guy, but a guy who wants to be a girl?"

Mike nods. "We could find out."

They look at each other. Then suddenly they grab me.

"Hey!" I try to break free, but they've got my arms pinned to my sides and they're half-dragging, half-shoving me into the boys' room. I let out a shriek, but it's too late. I'm inside, breathing in the smell of stale piss and urinal cakes, watching the door thump closed.

"Please," I whimper. I'm a pathetic sight. Frightened, humiliated, my knees weak and shaking. "Let me go."

"Not till we see what you got down there," Rory says. He reaches for the snap on my jeans and pops it open. I writhe in their arms, lift one knee to my stomach. Mike feels for the zipper.

Suddenly, the door opens and, like a spider in shining armor, Reilly Briggs walks in. Rory and Mike don't even notice, or maybe they don't care. I hear the metallic rip of my zipper coming down.

Reilly freezes when he sees us scuffling, backs up. Maybe I was wrong about the knight stuff. Don't leave, I pray. He clears his throat, and Rory and Mike turn around.

"It's D.J. Dork," Mike says.

"The white Jazzy Jeff," Rory chuckles. "Hey, man, where's the Fresh Prince?"

"What the hell's going on?" Reilly asks, glancing nervously at me.

"Why don't you use a different bathroom," Rory says. It's not a suggestion, it's an order.

Mike grabs my jeans and pulls them down. I'm too mortified to speak, to move. I'm just hunched over and shivering.

"Let her go or I'm going straight to the principal," Reilly says. No one moves. He turns and starts for the door.

"Oh, for Christ's sake," Rory groans. "What does it matter what's in John-John's pants? Male *or* female, I don't want to get near it."

Mike laughs. They exchange a glance, then release me and walk out the door, roughly shoving Reilly against the wall as they go. He hits hard and falls to his knees.

I pull up my pants and fumble with the zipper. All I'm thinking about is getting the hell out of there. I hurry past Reilly, who is picking himself up off the floor.

"You're Jeannie Holtz, right?" he asks.

I freeze, stare at the tiles. "Yeah."

He smiles. "There's definitely a rap in all this."

I don't answer, just grunt a sort of "thank you" and lunge out the door. But as I stumble back to study hall I'm thinking, Is he insane? How could I just turn what happened into a song? Besides, all I can think about is hacking Rory and Mike to bits with a meat cleaver.

As if I had the guts for something like that. I don't even have the guts to turn them in to the principal.

I was five years old when my mother enrolled me in ballet. My hatred started even before the first class, when Mom took me to the store to buy a pink leotard and shoes. I didn't want to try them on, and I definitely didn't want to pose for Daddy's camera with my hands over my head and a "big-girl smile" on my face.

At the first class Miss Stringfellow told us to dance like little flowers being blown in the breeze. I was a tree being ripped from the ground by a roaring hurricane. My mother, peering in through the tiny window in the door, looked mortified.

I refused to go to the second class. I threw a tantrum outside the door, eyes bloated, snot hanging from my nose, arms and legs flailing. Mom tried her soothing voice, her "babies cry; big girls use their words" speech, her best pained expression. Nothing worked.

The other mothers were staring. "Stop!" my mother hissed in my ear. "Do you hear me, Jeannie? Stop right this minute!"

Then she pinched me. Hard. I was so shocked, I stopped crying.

"That's a big girl," she said, suddenly all smiles. "Now let's go in."

She led me inside. I didn't cry after that. I just dragged myself through the class, head down, feet shuffling.

At lunch the next day Reilly's got his turntables set up and he's spinning and scratching. I sit nearby and he sees me. "You start on that rap?" he calls.

I just shrug. When the period ends, he comes over and sits beside me. "You wanna come over to my place this weekend?" he asks. "Maybe listen to some discs?"

Why is this guy being nice to me? Or does he just feel sorry for me? I murmur something noncommittal.

He writes his address on a piece of notebook paper. "I have to work Saturday. Come over Sunday afternoon." Then he gathers up his books and his record albums and walks away.

I'm not going to Reilly's. I can't. What would I say? What would I wear? What would we do?

Wait a minute, what am I thinking? I'm acting as if this is a date or something. Truth is, all Reilly wants out of me is a rap.

Okay, all the more reason not to go. I don't write raps, don't have a clue where to start.

Still, all day long, words, phrases, even some rhymes begin to percolate in my head. I don't know where they're coming from. I just wake up Saturday morning, and there they are.

Am I a girl, a boy, a lesbo, a fag?
I don't want a label, I don't need your tag.

I say the lines over and over in my head. After a while the next lines appear.

I'm a person, a human.
I need room and
a little respect,
To grow and connect,
Inspect, reject,
Find my place in this world,
Look for love, try sex.

I write it all down and read it over. Hmm, maybe I *can* write a rap song. But there's no way I'm going to show this stuff to Reilly. It's too personal, too painful. Besides, he'd probably decide I'm some kind of sicko.

So I sit down and write something I can show him, something that has nothing to do with me. It's a rap about black/white relations, about poverty and prejudice in the land of plenty. I think Reilly will like it.

Reilly lives in an apartment house near the river. "Come on in," he says. "My mom's at work, so there's no one to hassle us."

He doesn't mention his dad, so I figure maybe he isn't in the picture. He leads me to his room. There are records, CDs, tapes everywhere, on the floor, the bed, the desk, the shelves. His turntables and mike are set up in the middle of the room.

"Ms. Filbert says you're a poet," Reilly tells me, clearing aside some records to sit on the bed.

I'm alone with a guy, I think. In his room. How does that make you feel? I ask myself, like some psychiatrist in a movie. But I'm too choked up with nerves to feel anything.

"I don't know how to rap," I say. "But I wrote down a couple of lines."

My hand is trembling as I pull the paper from my pocket. It drops on the floor and Reilly snatches it. Oh, shit. The rap I want to read is on the front, but the original rap is scribbled on the back, plus some new rhymes I wrote down last night.

"Give it to me," I say, grabbing for the paper. "It won't sound right if I don't read it to you."

But Reilly turns his back to me and reads both sides. I stand there, cheeks burning, stomach churning. I want to run away and never look back.

Finally, he turns around, looks me over. "This 'straight outta Compton' stuff is pretty trite. But these other rhymes . . ." He taps the page and smiles. "I think I can do something with this."

Soon I'm spending almost every afternoon at Reilly's house. Mom doesn't ask where I am. She's too busy taking care of my father to even notice I'm gone.

Reilly puts beats behind my rhymes. He makes me read them into the microphone, over and over. He doesn't laugh at me, thank God, and he never mentions what he saw that day in the boys' room. All he says is: "Don't just read the words, Jeannie, *feel* them. Get pissed."

I shake my head and stare at the pattern on his Indian bedspread. I can write mad, but I can't let myself *be* mad. It's too scary.

The winter dance is coming up at school. They send a flyer home in our Friday folder.

"This looks fun," Mom says. "Let's buy you a new dress."

"I don't wear the old ones," I say.

"It's such a shame. You have wonderful legs. Like Daddy always tells me, 'If you have it, flaunt it.' And what about this hair? Can't I do something with—"

She reaches out to me, but I pull away. Our eyes meet and I notice that her eyeliner is crooked.

"They're taking Daddy to the hospital tomorrow," she says.

"What? *Why?*"

"He'll get much better care there. It's what he needs."

My throat aches, struggling to hold back the tears.

Mom touches my cheek. "Let's buy that new dress."

In the middle of the night the phone rings. I'm sure it's the hospital. My father is dead. When Mom walks into my room, I'm hiding under the covers, too scared to move. I hold my breath, listening for her sobs. Instead, I hear a smile in her voice as she says, "It's Chrissy."

Chrissy! We still write to each other once in a while, but I haven't spoken to her since she moved to the shore. I throw off the covers and grab the portable phone.

"Mom said no long-distance calls," Chrissy whispers, "so I waited until she was asleep."

"I can't believe it's you," I say. "I miss you so much."

"Me too. Listen, you'll never believe what happened. I went all the way!"

It takes me a second to figure out what she's talking about. Then I get it. She means sex. "Who with?" I ask.

"Mitch Bertofsky. I wrote to you about him, remember? We did it in the dunes. There was a full moon, the surf was pounding. It was incredible, Jeannie."

I feel so out of it. How can I tell her I still haven't been kissed?

"What about you, Jeannie?" she asks. "Are you seeing anyone?"

At least I don't have to lie about that, not really. "His name is Reilly. We're writing songs together."

"Songs! Since when are you a songwriter?"

"I'm writing the lyrics. They're raps, kind of."

She grills me on what Reilly looks like, sounds like, how he dresses, how he kisses. I get around that last part by simply saying he has great lips.

"Listen, Jeannie, my mom said I could invite you here for a long weekend. I'm supposed to write to you, but I couldn't wait. Can you come next weekend? There's a bus that stops in Toms River."

Will Chrissy still like me? What if she's totally into clothes and makeup and her new boyfriend? What if she takes one look at me and decides she's made a big mistake?

I'm scared, but I can't say no. I want to see her new house. I want to walk on the beach with her, swap secrets like we used to do, giggle in the dark. I want a friend.

I've been thinking a lot about Chrissy and her boyfriend. What would it be like to make love with a guy? Not just any guy, I mean. With Reilly.

I can't stop thinking about it. Does he like me? I wonder. It's hard to tell. When we're together, all we talk about is music. Do I like him? Yes, I do. But like *that?* I'm not sure.

The next day after school, I go over to his house. We work on my song. I've written a lot more rhymes over the last couple of weeks, and I've strung them together into something like a stream-of-consciousness poem. Reilly likes it, but he says I need a chorus. Not a rap, but a melody section with words that will tie the whole thing together.

"You need inspiration," he says. "Sit down. I'll play you one of my favorite songs."

He pops in a CD and I sit on the bed beside him. Marvin Gaye starts to sing, his voice smooth and sensuous. "What's going on, ah, what's going on . . ."

I can smell Reilly—a mixture of cotton, shampoo, and cinnamon. I can feel the warmth of his arm lying right next to mine. Maybe if he kissed me, I think, everything would make sense. Everything would be easy.

Without looking, without thinking, I reach over and grope for his hand. When he feels my skin touch his, he lets out a little gasp, then pulls away.

"Look, Jeannie, it's not . . ." His voice trails off. "I've been in bands with girls before." Pause. "We're on the verge of making some really powerful music here. Let's not do anything that might screw it up."

Oh, Christ, what was I thinking? That some guy would actually like me? Me, the overgrown tomboy with my baggy T-shirt, skinny kid body, and tangled hair. That was cute back in grade school, but now? It's just laughable, pathetic.

Reilly turns off the CD. He seems perfectly calm, as if nothing happened. Nothing important, anyway. "I'll lay down a beat," he says. "Just close your eyes and sing. Don't think, just do it. Whatever pops into your head."

But the only words that come are too painful to say. *I'm a freak, I'm a freak, I'm a freak.*

I feign a headache and leave. I'm not going back, not ever. After what happened, I can't face Reilly again.

I'm packing for Chrissy's house when Mom comes into my room. "I don't know if this is a good time for you to be going away," she says softly. "Daddy isn't doing well."

I don't want to hear that, not now. I've got to get out of here—away from my father's shriveling body, away from the lost look in my mother's eyes, away from Reilly Briggs.

"Mom, *please,* it's all arranged. Chrissy is expecting me."

She doesn't answer.

"Mom, come on. I haven't seen Chrissy for so long. Besides, it's just for the weekend. I'll be back Sunday night."

I can see her weakening.

"She's my best friend," I say. "My *only* friend."

"All right, if it means that much to you . . ."

I throw my arms around her. "Thanks, Mom! You're the best."

She smiles. I think it does her good to see me happy. At least that's what I tell myself.

Chrissy is into clothes, makeup, and boys, just like I was afraid she'd be. Still, she seems happy to see me. We talk a lot about the past, remembering all the crazy things we did and the trouble we got into. We walk on the beach, ignoring the icy wind, collecting seashells. She sets up a double date—her boyfriend and her, his best friend and me. We go to the movies. Chrissy spends the whole time making out with her boyfriend. His buddy and I watch the film.

Then on Sunday morning, the phone rings. Chrissy and I are still in bed, talking and giggling. Her mom walks into the room and shocks me by sitting on the bed and hugging me. I'm trying to figure out how to respond when she says, "That was your mother, Chrissy. Your father passed away late last night."

I can't take in the fact that my father is dead. It's like the Grand Canyon, too vast to comprehend. What hits me instead is that I let my mother down. She only asked one thing from me during the entire time my father was sick, and I refused her.

The funeral is later that week. Family friends, business associates of my father's, relatives—they all come up to me, put their arm around my shoulders, and whisper soothing words in my ear.

"Your father loved you very, very much."

"You look just like him."

"He was so proud of you."

Mom doesn't look at me. I want to take her hand, but I can't. I want to cry and scream and fall on my knees in front of her, but my feet are paralyzed and I'm unable to produce even one tear.

The winter dance is this weekend. Mom is still insisting that I go. It's the last thing in the world I want to do.

Reilly is going to be there, spinning discs. After what happened, I can't face him.

I let Mom take me to the store, buy me a dress I'd never pick for myself in a million years. It's black velvet with lacy snowflakes around the neck and sleeves. She picks out some black shoes to go with it.

At home I try on the dress and shoes. Mom looks really pleased. I force myself to smile, to push my hair out of my eyes. It's the least I can do for her.

It's the night of the dance and I'm standing outside the school in my new dress and shoes. Underneath, just to make me feel more comfortable, I'm wearing black bike shorts and a sleeveless black undershirt. I can hear the music pounding inside, hear the people talking and laughing. I want to run, but Mom's car is still idling at the curb and I know she's watching, waiting for me to go inside.

I shuffle into the lobby, thinking maybe I'll spend the evening in the restroom. But right away I spot Rory and Suzanne over by the trophy cabinet and I hurry into the gym to avoid them. Instead, I practically run into Mike Forelli.

"Whoa, look at Johnny," he tells his buddies. "Shake it, baby, shake it. Show us what you've got!"

Everyone laughs. I snake my way through the crowd of writhing bodies on the dance floor, putting some distance between Mike and me. I find a chair in the corner near the refreshment table and sit down. Nobody notices me. I close my eyes and let the music throb through me. I pretend I'm alone in my room.

Suddenly, I feel a hand on my shoulder. My eyes fly open and I'm face-to-face with Reilly.

"You wanna dance?" he asks.

I shake my head no.

"Talk?"

"No."

He looks at me, but his expression is inscrutable. Does he think I'm a pain in the butt? A pathetic geek? A self-impressed snob? Maybe all of the above. He walks away.

A band from the junior college, Boiling Point, gets up and plays a set of disco oldies. I'm wondering if it's too early to call my mother when finally the music ends and Reilly starts setting up his turntables, a tape deck, and a mike.

He told me at our second rehearsal that he wanted me to perform my rap tonight, but I said no. I knew I couldn't get up in front of the entire school and rap. I couldn't get up there period. I'd be too embarrassed, too self-conscious. Now it's a moot point. Our relationship—musical, personal, whatever—is over.

Reilly turns on the tape deck and plays a slow, soulful beat. With his long spider arms he tosses two records on the turntables and plays snippets of songs; then bends them, repeats them, slows them down and speeds them up. He's like a chef, combining dozens of everyday ingredients to make something new, something delicious.

Everyone is dancing, swaying to the beat. Reilly pops in a new cassette and the tempo speeds up. And suddenly I realize he's laying down the beat for my rap. The one we created together.

Reilly leans into the microphone. "Listen up, everyone. Jeannie Holtz is going to rap for us. Jeannie, get on up here."

Oh, my God. Everyone is looking at me. I can hear snickering. I'm just sitting there, staring at my feet, trying to will myself to disappear.

Someone starts to clap. "Jean-*nie!* Jean-*nie!*" Soon all the people in the gym are stamping their feet and chanting my name.

Someone grabs my hand and pulls me up. The crowd shoves me onto the stage. I want to die. Just curl up in a corner and die. Then I spot Rory and Mike at the front of the crowd. They're leering at me, relishing the chance to watch me make an ass of myself.

Reilly hands me the microphone. I'm still looking at Mike and Rory.

"Shake it, Johnny, shake it!" Mike taunts. "Come on, dyke. Show us what you've got."

That's when it happens. It's like a bomb going off inside of me, ripping me apart. I open my mouth and words explode into the air.

"Am I a girl, a boy, a lesbo, a fag?" I shout. "I don't want a label, I don't need your tag."

I'm glaring at Mike now, spitting out the words.

"I'm a person, a human.
I need room and
a little respect,
To grow and connect,
Inspect, reject,
Find my place in this world,
Look for love, try sex."

Everyone is staring at me, stunned—the kids, the teachers, the parent chaperones. But I barely notice. I'm thinking about my mother, my father, Reilly, the woman at the lesbian bookstore, Rory and Mike. All the confusion, the rejection, the mistakes, the longing, the pain.

I grab the front of my dress and pull as hard as I can. I feel the seams give way. I pull again and the material falls off me, revealing my bike shorts and undershirt. I take off my shoes and throw them into the crowd.

The music is changing now. This is the spot where Reilly wanted me to sing the chorus.

"I'm a freak," I sing in a low, soulful voice. It's a mournful lament. Then my voice rises. "I'm a freak, a freak, a freak!" It's a proclamation now, a joyful refrain. I jump up on the amplifier and spit out the next lines.

"You want to trash me, smash me,
Dis me and bash me.
Still I lower my head and I let you catch me.
Is it something in me,
That makes me freeze?
A fear of talking back,
Of showing feelings, I'm reeling,
I want to shout it to the ceiling:
I won't bow down, you won't catch me kneeling."

I prowl across the stage, filled with restless energy, unable to stop moving. I'm remembering those fantasies I had about blasting Rory and Mike away with a bazooka, poisoning them, hacking them apart with a meat cleaver. Now I'm doing it, only I'm using my voice to destroy them. I'm rapping, raving, raging, taking aim from somewhere deep in my soul.

"I'm a freak!" I moan, so alone, so sad. "I'm a freak!" I shriek, angry, violent. "I'm a freak, a freak, a freak!" I cry, so joyous, so complete.

And then it's over and there's silence, just silence until someone decides to clap. Soon everyone is applauding, cheering—some sincerely, some with ironic smiles on their faces because they think it's all a big joke. And I'm standing there in my bike shorts and undershirt, barefoot, the shredded dress at my feet, suddenly just me again—only different. Because for the first time in years, in centuries, in eons, I didn't stuff my emotions down inside of me. I was standing on the roof naked, screaming my lungs out, and it felt good.

I turn to leave the stage and feel arms closing around me. It's Reilly and he's hugging me. "You're incredible," he says in my ear. "I want to keep making music with you, Jeannie. Please say yes."

Well, it's a start, I tell myself, and then wonder, of what? A romance? A career? A life? I'm not sure exactly, but it feels right. I smile up into Reilly's sweet daddy longlegs face. "Okay," I say. "Yes."

Francess Lantz

Author of more than thirty books for young people, Francess Lantz admits she was a tomboy when she was younger. "I actually had short hair and dressed as a boy for several years," she says. Although she never questioned her sexuality as Jeannie does, growing up in Bucks County, Pennsylvania, wasn't easy for her. She played the guitar and expressed in songs the feelings she didn't have the courage to speak about. Lantz, who now lives with her husband and young son in Santa Barbara, California, used some of those old feelings in telling Jeannie's story.

Lantz's novels for middle-grade readers are *Neighbors from Outer Space*, *Spinach with Chocolate Sauce*, and *Stepsister from the Planet Weird*, which was a TV movie on the Disney Channel. Her nonfiction books include *Rock, Rap, and Rad: How to Be a Rock or Rap Star* and a how-to book for young actors, *Be a Star!*

Her young adult novel *Someone to Love*—an ALA Best Book for Young Adults and an IRA Young Adult Choice—is the story of the relationship between an unmarried, pregnant teenage girl and the fifteen-year-old daughter of the family that is going to adopt the teenager's baby. In *Fade Far Away* Lantz explores the strained relationship between an artistic fifteen-year-old girl and her famous sculptor father, who learns he is dying from a brain tumor. Her latest work is a three-book teen romance series entitled *You're the One!*

You can learn more about Fran Lantz and her books at www.silcom.com/~writer, or you can contact her directly by E-mail at writer@silcom.com.

Ms. Noonan

Graham Salisbury

It was bad enough that Billy Keiffer had to deal with Nitt and Johnson, two seniors who took pleasure in making him miserable. But when Mrs. Noonan entered his life, more trouble came his way than he ever thought possible.

HE'D SEEN Mrs. Noonan before, of course.

She was his chemistry teacher's wife. He'd seen her coming and going from their small faculty house. Sometimes he would see her working in her garden or carrying something in from her car, or maybe just out walking with Mr. Noonan.

But this time it was different.

Billy Keiffer was in tenth grade—a freaky year, maybe even the freakiest year of his entire life so far. At his all-boy boarding school up in the island high country, the air on a clear night was often cool and crisp.

On this particular night Keiffer was out in the cow pasture hiding from Nitt and Johnson. He'd found a place just outside the fence that separated the school from the ranch that edged it. He'd flattened a square of tall grass and was lying on his back with his hands behind his head, thinking of ways he could get Nitt, and Johnson too, for that matter—make their lives as miserable as they'd been making his.

Within ten minutes he figured he'd spent about enough brain cells on those two idiots. Forget them, he thought. My time will come, and when it does I'll know what to do. Sooner or later Nitt will pay. Oh, yeah, he's going to pay, all right.

Keiffer dozed a moment, then opened his eyes.

Wow, he thought. Look at the stars. Look how incredibly many there are. Billions.

He listened to the night.

Only a few mosquitoes.

Nothing moved, nothing at all; there wasn't even a breath of breeze.

He bolted up.

What if someone came looking for him? They might. If Mr. Bentley went to his room for some reason. And he wasn't there.

Keiffer peeked over the tall grass.

That's when he saw . . .

Oh.

He hadn't realized he was that close to the faculty bungalows. He stopped breathing.

She was so . . .

Close.

Keiffer gulped in air. He felt his heart leaping up into his throat. His body trembled like a wet dog's.

Oh, oh, oh.

The grassy spot was at the top of a small rise that sloped down toward the house. Not forty yards away, framed within the warm yellow square of a window, was Mrs. Noonan. And Keiffer could see perfectly.

She must have turned the light on while he'd been thinking about Nitt, or maybe while he'd dozed off.

She was reading.

Keiffer sank down to where he could just see up over the grass.

She was sitting at one end of a navy blue couch with her legs tucked up under her. A floor lamp illuminated her golden hair. Keiffer already knew her name was Julie. Mr. Noonan had told them that in class. Keiffer guessed she was about twenty-six, since Mr. Noonan was twenty-six. He'd told them that too.

She smiled as she read, one hand holding the book, the other tucked into the fold of her evening kimono, just above her breast.

Keiffer's hands were more than trembling now.

Shaking.

It was an accident.

Really. Being there looking into Mr. Noonan's window at his wife was not something he'd come out here to do. He'd only wanted to get away from Nitt and Johnson.

He had to leave.

Now.

But he couldn't move. He couldn't turn away.

Mrs. Noonan took her hand from her kimono to swipe the corner of her eye with a finger. Whatever she was reading was making her smile and cry at the same time. She put her hand back where it had been, inside her kimono.

The vision burned itself into Keiffer's brain.

The window.

The blue sofa.

Her glowing hair.

Her hand.

Mr. Noonan suddenly came into the room.

Keiffer fell back into the grass. He got back up. He'd never seen Mr. Noonan in his pajamas before. Not really pajamas, but a T-shirt and boxer shorts. Mr. Noonan stood behind the sofa with his hand on Mrs. Noonan's shoulder. He leaned down and kissed the top of her head.

Keiffer knew he should get out of there. What he was doing wasn't right. But he couldn't turn away from it, not in a million years.

Mrs. Noonan looked up, smiling. She touched Mr. Noonan's hand, took it and kissed it.

Kissed it and pulled it down.

Keiffer stumbled back. He scrambled to his feet and ran, his heartbeat slamming up in his throat.

Three nights later in the dorm, Nitt and Johnson put centipedes in Keiffer's bed, and in his roommate Casey's. Casey got stung and screamed like a girl. Keiffer ran out the door, thinking the place was infested.

Nitt and Johnson were in the hall, laughing their heads off, rolling on the floor and holding their stomachs.

"You're sick, you stupid freaks!" Keiffer shouted.

Inside the room, Casey screamed again.

Johnson was crying with laughter.

Nitt, trying to stand, pointed at Keiffer. He was practically crying too, he was laughing so hard. "You're the freak, Keiffer. You're such a fairy," he said.

Keiffer charged and slammed into him with his shoulder, knocking him to the floor. Nitt landed flat on his back. "Ooof!"

For a moment Nitt couldn't breathe, the air knocked out of him. He sat and stared up in wide-eyed panic. His face started turning red.

Johnson grabbed Keiffer by the neck and threw him out of the way. Keiffer hated Nitt but he was terrified of Johnson. Keiffer once saw Johnson put a safety pin through the skin on his own arm, grinning at the guys who were watching him. He clipped the pin shut and wore it on his arm until it got infected.

Johnson knelt and thumped Nitt's back. A few long seconds later Nitt caught his breath and gasped.

"You better start running, Keiffer," Johnson said.

Nitt struggled to his knees, his eyes cold. He staggered up, fat fists balled. He stood nearly a foot taller than Keiffer.

"Stay away from me!" Keiffer shouted. They could kill him if they wanted, he didn't care, just get it over with.

Nitt grinned. "You're gonna pay for that, homo."

Every door in the hall was open now, heads peeking out.

Nitt struck so quickly that Keiffer didn't even see it coming. The blow caught him on the side of his head. He stumbled back and fell. White stars speckled his vision and his ears rang.

Nitt kicked him in the stomach and stood over him, a bomb ready to go off if Keiffer said one more word.

Keiffer sat balled up, his hand covering his ear.

Someone yanked Nitt away. All Keiffer saw was a hand grabbing Nitt's shoulder and spinning him around.

"That's enough," Casey said. "I'm getting Mr. Bentley."

Nitt shoved Casey away. "Don't touch me, you faggot!"

Casey backed away and ran down the hall.

"Yeah, go get Mommy," Johnson called after him.

Nitt kicked Keiffer again. "You haven't seen anything yet, Keiffie-babes."

Nitt and Johnson walked away as Casey banged on the dorm master's door. Mr. Bentley wasn't in.

Keiffer waited three nights before sneaking out again. He waited until Casey was asleep. Casey always dozed off before lights out, which was ten o'clock. He was one of those guys who could get straight A's without opening a book, almost.

Keiffer crept through the bushes, staying in the shadows out behind the mess hall. His hands started to tremble with anticipation of what he might see. Mrs. Noonan lived with him, now, in his mind. He could hardly think of anything else.

He made his way around in back of the faculty bungalows. He found the grassy spot, still mashed down.

But the light in the Noonans' house was off.

His hands stopped trembling. The fantasies began to fade. But he kept hoping.

He waited fifteen minutes and was just about to leave when the light flicked on. And there, in the window, there, there . . .

Julie.

This time her kimono was loosely hung about her. Keiffer was stunned. What is this? What is this feeling, this monster feeling?

He nearly had a heart attack when she came to the window, bent down, and looked directly at him.

He froze, stupefied.

But she was only unlatching the window so she could raise it an inch or two.

She sat again on the couch with her book. She opened it, and with her free hand gathered up the looseness in the kimono.

Mr. Noonan didn't appear this time. Keiffer stayed until she turned the light off, an hour later, or thereabouts.

Nothing stirred in the dorm when he returned. Casey still lay as he'd been, facing the wall, dead to the world.

Keiffer fell asleep at about two in the morning, after reliving every memory he could drag up about Mrs. Noonan.

Julie Noonan.

Beautiful Julie Noonan.

A night later he went again. She was lying on the couch talking on the phone.

When he went again two nights after that, the house was dark. He waited nearly an hour, but nothing happened. He knew he shouldn't go there every night, but he couldn't help it. The next night she was there, alone, reading.

His favorite dream was that he was lying on the couch with his head in her lap, and as she read, she stroked his hair and his cheek, leaning down every so often to kiss him. He dreamed about her when he was outside her window. He dreamed about her before falling asleep, and sometimes even had real dreams that were wilder and better than his daydreams. He dreamed of her in the mess hall when he was at lunch or dinner, looking across the tables to where she sat next to Mr. Noonan.

He went out again that Sunday night.

He could have avoided trouble if he'd been even half-alert, but everything around him was consumed in a blur of anticipation.

He was passing behind the mess hall.

"Fairy," someone whispered from the darkness.

He immediately dropped to a squat.

"Yeah, you, Keiffie-babes. What you doing out here?"

Keiffer saw an orange-red glow of light.

A cigarette.

No, two cigarettes.

"Come here," Nitt whispered.

Keiffer stood and walked toward the back of the mess hall. He saw two shadows with red glows, leaning against the side of the building. Johnson and Nitt.

Keiffer squinted. It looked like Johnson was scanning the stars with a pair of binoculars.

"Come on," Nitt said. "We don't bite."

If he ran he might make it back to the dorm before they caught him. But maybe not too, and if he did run, and they did catch him, it would be worse than just doing what they said.

Panic flared up and inhabited Keiffer's entire body. What if they'd seen him sneaking around before and had been waiting for him? He didn't think they had, but it was possible. Or were they just out stealing a smoke? He'd have to be way more careful in the future.

Nitt and Johnson stood sucking their cigarettes, the embers glowing, then dimming. Nitt flicked his away. It twirled into the darkness and vanished.

"Come closer," he said, softly.

Keiffer took a step.

"Two bits says you were on your way to the pasture, huh? Going out to run naked in the night." He chuckled. "That right?"

"No."

"No?"

He turned to Johnson. "You hear that? The fairy just came out here to go nowhere."

Johnson said nothing, still studying the stars with the binoculars. He sucked his cigarette. "Look at that," he said.

Nitt glanced up. "Satellite."

"Closest thing to a UFO we've seen yet."

Keiffer saw the white pinprick moving across the sky in a pure, clean arc.

Johnson put the binoculars down. "I heard they do that, you know, run naked . . . the fairy guys."

Nitt snickered. "That's really it, isn't it, Keiffie-babes?"

Keiffer said nothing. He should have run when he had the chance.

He bolted.

But they were faster.

Nitt grabbed his T-shirt. Keiffer tried to squirm away, but Johnson was all over him. They threw him to the ground, facedown, and sat on him.

Nitt whispered in his ear. "Where you going, homo? The party's just warming up."

They turned him over. Nitt unbuttoned Keiffer's jeans and yanked them off. Johnson pulled his T-shirt up over his head and threw it into the weeds.

Nitt, sitting on Keiffer's knees, said to Johnson, "You pull off his underpants. I ain't touching it."

Johnson grinned. "Stand up, faggot."

Keiffer sat, then got to his feet.

"Take 'em off," Johnson said.

Keiffer stared at Johnson. I won't cry, he willed, won't, won't. He bent over and removed his underwear. The burn in his throat swelled. Cry, cry. He crammed it back down inside him.

"Throw them on the roof," Johnson said.

Keiffer tossed his underpants up on top of the mess hall.

"Cute," Nitt said to Johnson.

"Thanks."

It was dark. So what if he was naked? He could make it back to the dorm without being seen. Just wait, and run when the chance came.

"Hold this little pecker's arms up over his head," Nitt said, whispering, trying to keep his voice down.

Johnson grabbed Keiffer's wrists and pulled his arms up. "Ow!" Keiffer said, trying to wiggle free.

Johnson kneed Keiffer in the butt, and Keiffer stopped.

"I need your weed," Nitt said, taking the cigarette from Johnson's lips. He took a deep drag on it, the tip red hot. Then he pointed the small fire at Keiffer's face. He grinned, then moved the burning tip down to

Keiffer's armpit. He held it so close Keiffer could feel the heat.

"You tell anyone we did this to you and we'll make this part real. Can you imagine it? The stink of burning flesh? The pain in your foul armpit?"

Keiffer said nothing.

"You understand, Keiffie-babes?"

"Yes," Keiffer squeaked.

"Let him go," Nitt said.

Keiffer rubbed his wrists. He felt like a ghost in his nakedness. He bent over, crossed his hands over his crotch.

"What you got to hide, sweetheart? Fairies don't have dongs."

Johnson stifled a laugh.

"What'd you do with my binoculars?" Nitt asked.

Johnson picked them up, brushed the dirt off, and handed them to Nitt.

Nitt packed them into a case and threw the strap over his shoulder. "Let's go," he said.

They took Keiffer out into the pasture. He could see Mr. Noonan's house. The light was on, but no one was in sight. Keiffer turned away quickly, not wanting Nitt or Johnson to even have a clue about the window. Oh, God, what they would do if they knew about Mrs. Noonan.

Nitt stopped out in the middle of the pasture. "This should do, huh, Keiffie?"

Keiffer glanced around to see if there were any cows, or worse, bulls. But he could see only dark shadows of trees and bushes and the few lights on campus.

"We're going to be watching," Nitt said. "And we're going to be real disappointed if you don't have a good time out here, you know? So just go on and play with yourself, fairybabes, flit around like Tarzan or Peter Pan or whoever it is you want to be."

He tapped Keiffer's shoulder, as if they were good old buds from way back.

They left, their laughter slicing the stillness.

Keiffer noticed for the first time that he was cold. He crossed his arms. What do I do? What?

He looked back toward the school, the faculty bunga-lows.

Oh, no, now she was there.

In the window.

Keiffer felt a crybaby-burn rise in his throat again. Tears spilled from his eyes. He wiped them away quickly.

Crouching low, he made his way back, slipping around the mess hall the opposite way. It meant he would have to sprint across the quad to get to the dorm, out in the open. But he'd have to take that chance. Nitt might be waiting if he went back the way he'd come.

Keiffer stood at the edge of the building, half in the bushes. No one was in sight. He stepped out, started creeping into the quad.

"What the hell are you doing out here, Mr. Keiffer?"

Keiffer's heart nearly flew out of his throat. He stag-gered back. Mr. Bentley was sitting on the mess hall steps.

"I . . . I . . ."

Mr. Bentley stood. "Jesus, you're stark naked."

"But—"

At that moment Nitt and Johnson came out of the shadows behind Mr. Bentley. They stopped short, and ditched their cigarettes the second they saw him.

Mr. Bentley turned.

Nitt shot Keiffer a glare that said, If you breathe one word about anything you'll be dead in an hour.

"What the hell is going on here?" Mr. Bentley said. "Have you all gone mad? No one's supposed to be out of the dorm after ten. You know that."

Nitt, in his most agreeable voice, said, "We've just got senioritis, Mr. Bentley. You know how that is, don't you?"

Mr. Bentley shook his head.

Keiffer wondered if Nitt thought Mr. Bentley might have seen the cigarettes. Nitt said, "We were just playing a joke on Keiffer, sir."

Mr. Bentley looked at Keiffer. "Taking him outside buck naked, you mean?"

"Yeah, just a little joke."

Mr. Bentley eyed Nitt. "Mr. Nitt, you're so full of shit you're actually funny. Get the hell back to the dorm, all of you. Jesus."

Keiffer ran ahead. If stupid Nitt thought his butt was saved, he could think again. All Keiffer needed was time and a killer idea. Oh, yeah. Time and a killer idea.

The following Saturday night everyone was in the common room watching some old movie. Keiffer, Nitt, and Johnson sat in the library with their books spread out around them. Mr. Bentley had written them up for two hours of study hall as punishment. Thankfully, Mr. Bentley had kept the nakedness part to himself.

Keiffer sat alone at one of the computer tables, the lit screen blank in front of him. He had to write a report on Pearl Harbor for history. Nitt and Johnson were studying at tables of their own, farther away. But Keiffer could see them from where he sat. Two seventh graders were at another table. Mr. Paine, this week's study hall monitor, was at a desk up toward the door, keeping an eye on things.

Keiffer typed, *On December 7, 1941, the Japanese attacked Pearl Harbor.*

He stopped and thought.

And thought.

Of Mrs. Noonan.

It was hopeless. He was hopeless.

He peeked up at Mr. Paine, then over at Nitt, whose head was resting on his arms, folded over the top of the desk. Johnson was slouched down reading some book.

Keiffer opened a new page on the screen.

He typed, *Dear Julie.*

He peeked up again. He could feel a tingling inside him just at the thought of writing her a letter. He'd never give it to her, of course. But just to write it . . .

I know you don't know me, but you've probably seen me around. Who I am doesn't matter. What does matter is that I think you are the most beautiful woman I have ever seen in my life. I think about you every night and every day. I can't STOP. It's like I'm in a dream and you and I are the only people in the world. Sometimes I think about kissing you. I've never kissed anyone in my life. But if I could kiss you, I would never want to kiss anyone else ever again. I love you more

than anyone ever could. I don't know how to say it any
stronger than that. I love you, I love you, I love you.
    From your secret admirer

Keiffer read it, and smiled. He read it again and again.
He looked up. Nitt was still dozing and Johnson still
reading. He hit the print command and held his breath
as the printer hummed it out. He snatched it up and
read it one more time, then folded it and hid it in the
pages of his math book for later.

The next night in the dorm after dinner, when all the
kids were in their rooms doing homework, Keiffer
leaned back in his chair and stretched.

Casey was reading a novel in Spanish, lying on his bed
with headphones on. Probably listening to jazz, Keiffer
thought. Casey was a little weird, but a nice guy. He kept
to himself. Avoided trouble. All he wanted in the world
was to get into MIT with a perfect record.

Keiffer stood and Casey looked up.

"Just going out for a walk," Keiffer said. "I'm falling
asleep."

Casey nodded and turned back to his book.

Keiffer went a different way this time, skirting the
back of the mess hall. It was full dark out, no moon. The
air was cool and it smelled like ginger.

And she was there, alone in the room.

Keiffer figured Mr. Noonan must have a different
place in the house where he worked, or read, or graded
papers. Mrs. Noonan was talking on the phone again.
She wore a T-shirt this time and Keiffer wondered if she
had anything on under it. In his mind she didn't. He

remembered the letter he'd written and thought of how he'd felt as he'd written it and how it was true to the last drop. He should give it to her. Secretly.

A mosquito hummed near his ear and he slapped it. Whack!

Mrs. Noonan looked up.

She reached toward the lamp and shut it off.

Keiffer froze and stared at the darkened house.

A light appeared, a flashlight shining through the screen. Mumbling voices.

Keiffer staggered back and stumbled away. He fell and got up and raced through the weeds and grass and trees, sprinting back to the dorm and his room, where he slammed the door and leaned back against it, then fell on his bed, gasping.

Casey, still reading, looked up.

"Just . . . just ran a bit," Keiffer said. ". . . To wake up."

Casey shook his head.

A moment later he said, "Your friend Nitt was here looking for you."

Keiffer didn't answer. Immediately he got up and checked his stash to see if Nitt had taken his cookies that his mom had sent. There had been fourteen left. Now there were only five.

"He also messed around over at your desk," Casey added.

Keiffer checked there too. Everything was out of place, but nothing seemed to be missing. "What did he want?" he asked.

"What does he ever want? Food."

Keiffer scowled and straightened his desk. His hands

still shook from the shock of almost getting caught. He had no idea, just no idea, that sound could carry so far in the night outside Mrs. Noonan's window.

It took him hours to fall asleep. Moments after he finally did, he bolted awake. He turned on his desk lamp and grabbed his math book.

The letter was gone.

On Tuesday Keiffer took the biggest chance he'd ever taken in his life. It was so big that he wondered what was happening to him. He'd never acted this way before. He'd *thought* about doing things like this, many times, but he'd never actually followed up on anything.

This time he did.

Because the killer idea had arrived.

He pretended to be sick and spent the day in bed. But while everyone was at class, he crept over to the senior dorm and went into Nitt and Johnson's room. Nothing was ever locked. Which in this case was great. He had to find that letter and tear it up.

The room stank. It was like Nitt and Johnson had a stash of really gross laundry somewhere.

Keiffer couldn't find the letter.

In fact, Nitt had nothing at all of interest on or in his desk or clothes drawers or closet. He didn't even have one picture of anyone on his corkboard. He didn't have a stereo, a clock, or even a pencil sharpener. Keiffer frowned.

But there was the one other thing he'd come to get. And that was way more than enough.

Nitt's binoculars.

They were high up on the top shelf of Nitt's closet in their frayed black case. Someone had scribbled NITT, U.S. ARMY INFANTRY on the strap.

Keiffer grabbed the case and left.

That night, after he heard Casey breathing deeply, Keiffer threw the binocular case over his shoulder and peeked out into the quiet hall.

One light was on down near Mr. Bentley's apartment.

He hurried to the door and went out into the night feeling an electric thing inside him even stronger and more driving than before. It raced through him. Charged every nerve in his body so that the trembling in his hands took hold again, and even before he'd gotten halfway to the grassy hiding place outside Mrs. Noonan's window, he had to stop and breathe.

Breathe and think.

All right, settle down.

He gripped the binoculars.

She was reading.

She was wearing the kimono.

Keiffer couldn't keep the eyepiece still.

Wow.

Wow, wow, wow.

She was even more beautiful up close—so close that he kissed her, tasted her lips, felt them so soft and damp and smooth, her hands now caressing his face and hair.

Keiffer watched her read for fifteen minutes, exploring every inch of her—her eyes, her smile, her hair, her body, everything—until she put her hand inside her kimono above her breast, as was her habit.

When she did that, put her hand there, in that spot,

Keiffer lowered the binoculars. His ears quivered with the pain of it all. He could never have her to himself. Never. She loved Mr. Noonan. Not him. She would hate him if she knew he was out there spying. She would think he was nothing but some sick, dorky tenth grader.

"But it's not like that," he whispered.

He looked one more time, then lowered the binoculars and put them down in the grass, near the case.

Do it now, he thought.

He coughed, very lightly, as if trying to stifle it.

The light in the house went out.

In seconds Mr. Noonan burst out the back door with the flashlight, combing the trees and pasture, the beam passing just over Keiffer's head.

"Who's out there?" Mr. Noonan shouted.

When the beam moved off into the pasture, Keiffer got up and ran for his life.

The next morning Nitt got called into the headmaster's office. At noon in the mess hall word spread like floodwater. Nitt had been peeping into Noonan's house at night. More than once, everyone whispered. Mrs. Noonan had heard him out there. Mr. Noonan had found his binoculars.

That afternoon Keiffer was trying to concentrate in English class when a seventh grader came in with a note. Mr. Ellis read it, then strolled down the aisle to the back of the room and gave it to Keiffer.

Keiffer opened it.

He looked at it and sat for a moment without moving,

then stood and gathered his books. All eyes watched him leave.

He stepped out under gray and white clouds. Rain fell like mist as he headed across the green grass toward the headmaster's office.

Mr. Noonan was there. And Mr. Bentley. And Mr. Toms, the headmaster, a burly, red-haired man who rarely smiled.

Mr. Toms pointed to a chair and Keiffer sat. His hands started to tremble. He sat on them.

He'd been caught. It was over.

He waited for someone to say something.

To call his parents.

To tell him to go back to his room and start packing.

It was so quiet that he could hear Mr. Toms breathing.

Mr. Bentley leaned forward, his elbows on his knees. In one hand he held a folded piece of paper.

"Mr. Keiffer," he said, then paused.

Keiffer stared at the floor.

"I assume you've heard what happened with Mr. Nitt."

"Yes, sir."

Mr. Bentley nodded. "When we went through his belongings we found something that he swore was yours. He said he took it from your room."

Mr. Bentley handed Keiffer the folded paper. "Did you write this?"

Keiffer took the letter. He unfolded it and pretended to read it. He willed his hand to stop trembling.

The letter shook.

"Mr. Keiffer?"

"No, sir, this isn't mine. I don't know anyone named Julie."

Keiffer kept his eyes on the letter, afraid to look up. He felt sick.

Mr. Bentley went on. "Remember the night I caught you out buck naked?"

Keiffer winced. He wanted to crawl out of the room. He could feel the blood rush to his face.

"Yes, sir," he whispered.

"I've got to say, I was rather stunned to see you like that. But then Mr. Nitt and Mr. Johnson showed up and said they'd just played a practical joke on you. Was that true, what they said? Did they strip you and take you outside?"

"Yes, sir, they did. They took me out into the cow pasture."

"And . . ."

Keiffer looked up. He shrugged. "Nothing. I just walked back. That's when . . . when I saw you."

"Those two boys do that kind of thing to you a lot?"

"No, sir. I mean they never did that before. They do plenty of . . . of other stuff, but not that."

"What other stuff?"

"Beat me up. Steal food. Put centipedes in my bed."

Mr. Bentley paused, thinking.

Keiffer glanced up.

Mr. Bentley straightened and turned to Mr. Toms and Mr. Noonan. "Well, you know how the boys are. It's not the first time something like that has happened."

Keiffer glanced at Mr. Toms, who sat with his arms crossed, scowling, tapping a finger on his arm. "What's your point, Mr. Bentley," Mr. Toms said.

"My point is that Mr. Nitt has had it in for Mr. Keiffer for some time. Mr. Keiffer's roommate told me about the centipedes. I've no reason to believe that trying to pin the letter on Mr. Keiffer was any different. Besides, I just can't see Mr. Keiffer writing something like that. And we did find it in Mr. Nitt's room."

Mr. Toms, his arms still crossed, looked directly into Keiffer's eyes. He was mulling something over.

Finally, he said, "Did you write that letter, son?"

Keiffer felt as if his mind were a total blank. The thoughts and words he needed to tell the truth were just not there. Part of him wanted to get it out, get the whole thing over. But a stronger part of him was terrified.

"I don't know anyone named Julie," he mumbled.

Mr. Bentley sat back in his chair.

Mr. Noonan's silence was almost too much for Keiffer to bear.

"I'm going to ask you one more time, son," Mr. Toms said. "Is that letter yours? This is very important. Expelling a boy from this school is no small thing. Now, I want you to tell me—did Mr. Nitt take that letter from your room like he said he did?"

Keiffer's thoughts raced.

He saw, in his mind, the hot cigarette nearly burning his armpit, and he saw himself stripped naked in the pasture. He saw Nitt kicking him in the hallway, and the hate and rage in his eyes. He saw him shoving Casey and calling him a homo. And the cookie box with the missing cookies, and the centipedes in his bed, and the stolen letter, his letter, his, the private one he wrote that was meant for no one else to see but himself, no one, ever.

"Son?"

Keiffer could not speak. He was gone. He knew it. Gone, gone, gone. He'd pack tonight probably. Call his mom.

There was a long silence.

He'd tell them the truth.

Keiffer felt himself swaying, just slightly. He could hardly keep from passing out.

Tell them.

Keiffer shook his head. "No, sir. I did not write that letter."

Mr. Toms studied him. A long, thoughtful look.

Finally, he said, "I'm inclined to believe you."

Keiffer looked up, then down. Then up.

Mr. Toms breathed deeply, thinking. He rubbed a hand over his face. A truck shifted gears out on the road, the sound of the engine falling, then rising again.

Mr. Toms stood. "You can go, Mr. Keiffer."

Keiffer stayed where he was.

Tell him, he thought. Tell him now.

Keiffer stood, and left the room.

In less than twenty-four hours Nitt was history.

Put on a plane to Honolulu.

Expelled.

For days Keiffer felt awful. He didn't know what he'd meant to do, but getting Nitt kicked out of school wasn't part of it. He'd just wanted to . . . to get him. That's all. Just get him.

And he did, better than he'd ever imagined, and that felt good.

Yes?

No, it didn't.

He would tell. To lie was wrong.

But what did it matter anymore? He was going crazy

anyway. He was already a whack. Mrs. Noonan had made him that way.

All right, he decided. I'll do it. I'll tell. Just not right now. But soon.

Keiffer kept to himself more than ever after that, going a little crazier every day, he thought. His life was one big mess. He waffled back and forth many times a day: tell, now. No, it's done, let it be.

But above all else—he had to get Mrs. Noonan out of his mind. If it hadn't been for her none of this would have happened.

He stopped eating for a while. Then started again, nibbling. Never laughed or smiled. Never tried to talk to anyone. Just sank down into himself.

And, eventually, he even began to stop dreaming about Mrs. Noonan.

But then . . .

He was outside in the quad one sunny afternoon when he saw Mr. and Mrs. Noonan walking toward him. They were holding hands.

Maybe his mind was playing tricks on him, but Keiffer thought Mr. Noonan seemed to have taken on a new way of looking at him since that meeting in Mr. Toms's office. It was really weird, because Keiffer thought it was a look of admiration, almost as if Mr. Noonan respected him for having had the guts to talk with Mr. Toms the way he had. Stand up to Nitt's lie like he did.

Even so, Keiffer found it almost impossible to look Mr. Noonan in the eye. He'd glance at him and turn away quickly. That's how it usually went.

As he and Mrs. Noonan approached, Mr. Noonan smiled at Keiffer.

They stopped.

"How's it going, Keiffer?" Mr. Noonan said.

"All right."

"Staying out of trouble?"

"Yes, sir."

Mr. Noonan grinned and tapped Keiffer's shoulder. "Good man. Say, have you ever met my wife? I know you've seen her around, but I don't think you've actually met, have you?"

Keiffer shook his head. "No, sir."

He couldn't look at Mrs. Noonan either.

Just seeing her reminded him of Nitt, and his own private letter, the one Mr. Toms had in his desk drawer. Just thinking that made him cringe. No, he couldn't look at her. Mrs. Noonan was a bad dream for him now.

"Well, then," Mr. Noonan said. "Julie, meet Billy Keiffer. He's a fine young man and not a bad chemist."

"Hi, Billy," she said.

Her voice so soothing.

Saying his name.

So soft and light.

He forced himself to look up.

She was smiling, her head tilted slightly. She reached out to shake hands.

Keiffer hesitated, then took her hand.

Took Mrs. Noonan's hand.

The hand.

There was nothing else in the world now.

Absolutely nothing.

Graham Salisbury

Although he now lives in Portland, Oregon, Graham Salisbury grew up in the Hawaiian Islands, where his family has lived since 1820. The Islands provide the setting for all of his novels and short stories.

Like the characters in "Mrs. Noonan," Graham Salisbury attended a boarding school fifty miles from his home in Kailua-Kona. It was there, in the spectacular windy green highlands of Hawaii's cattle ranch country, that he learned how cruel some boys can be. He also daydreamed a lot, he admits, usually about girls. But, he says, "If 'Mrs. Noonan' had happened to me, I would have surely up and died. My daydreams would have quantum leaped to some gloriously wild and forbidden kingdom. I'd have been out there a ways. And I may not have come back, either. Hoo boy."

Before becoming a published author, Graham Salisbury worked as a deckhand on a deep-sea charter fishing boat, skippered a glass-bottom tourist boat, carved Hawaiian tikis with a hammer and chisel, taught elementary school, was a graphic artist, was a member of the classic rock band Millennium, earned a bachelor's degree from California State University, Northridge, and an MFA from Vermont College of Norwich University.

His novels—*Blue Skin of the Sea*, *Under the Blood-Red Sun*, *Shark Bait*, and *Jungle Dogs*—have together earned more awards than can be fit in the space available here.

His World War II novel, *Under the Blood-Red Sun*, for example, was an American Library Association Best Book for Young Adults and an ALA Notable Book, as well as a *Parent's Choice* Honor Award winner, an Oregon Book Award winner, winner of the Scott O'Dell Award for Historical Fiction, and a recipient of Hawaii's Nene Award and the California Young Reader's Medal. Salisbury also has received the Judy Lopez Memorial Award for Children's Literature and the PEN/Norma Klein Award.

You can find more details about Graham Salisbury and his books at **www.grahamsalisbury.com**.

WWJD

Will Weaver

Being a transfer student is difficult enough, but Suzanne also carries other burdens into her new high school. When counseling and drug therapy don't help, Suzanne's religious beliefs give her strength. However, her major tormentor, Eddie Halvorsen, won't give up.

LIKE JESUS, I am surrounded by sin. Every morning on my way to school I walk past rough boys with shaved heads and girls with pierced faces. They stand inches off the high school property line and smoke cigarettes. In the snow they stomp their feet to keep warm, and spit tobacco juice. When I appear, they whoop and swear and throw their trash at me. Every morning I am their amusement. Their victim.

I could easily avoid my tormentors by taking a different path from my aunt's house. But I try to live by one rule: WWJD. What would Jesus do? And the answer is clear. Jesus never took the easy way out. He never avoided the sinners, the lost, the lonely, the hurting. Rather, He went among them.

Today I carry a black plastic garbage bag. My antagonists do not see me immediately—two of them are wrestling in the snow. The rest are laughing and egging them on. I tighten my long orange scarf around my throat, and quietly I ease behind them. I begin to pick up their trash.

"Hey look, it's Weird Suzy!"

The two wrestlers, covered with dirt and snow, sit up to stare.

"Weird Suzy, Weird Suzy!" they all begin to chant.

Sticks and stones. Their name-calling does not bother me. After all, my real name is Suzanne, as in the Leonard Cohen song by the same name. I am a sixteen-year-old sophomore at River Forks High School in central Wisconsin, and the year is 2001. But I don't feel like this is my school, Wisconsin my state, or these times my times. I mentioned these feelings to the school counselor; after all, she asked how things were going for me. "Transfer students often feel a sense of alienation," she said. "And in any case, high school here in Wisconsin must be very different than in California."

"Not really," I said. "And anyway, I've felt strange most of my life."

She made me see a psychiatrist.

I tried to explain to the doctor that ever since I can remember I've felt odd. As if I were not like the other kids. "It might be because of my mother," I told him. But he was scribbling something on a little pad and I don't think he heard me. He smiled. "Go on, Suzanne," he said. As I talked, his eyes went briefly to his wristwatch.

When I finished, he smiled again and ripped off the little sheet of paper. "Tazamix," he said. "Fifteen milligrams, a very light dose. Trust me, Suzanne. After a week you'll feel way less anxious about things. You'll feel like you fit right in here at River Forks."

"Okay," I said. After all, he was the doctor.

Taking Tazamix was like putting on somebody else's glasses. The world was suddenly large and looming. Everything had straighter angles, sharper lines. Skin was cardboard; wood was metal. Butter knives felt razor sharp. Everything scared me. I waited up until my aunt finished her graveyard shift at the restaurant, and I told her how I was feeling.

"Suzy, honey, you flush those pills down the toilet right now!" she said. "Those shrinks are all crazy. Why do you think they became shrinks in the first place?"

I stopped taking the pills. In three or four days my world got smaller, with softer edges, just the way I liked it.

This morning a can of Mountain Dew clatters at my feet. Yellow spray splashes my clothes, spatters my face.

"Good hit, Eddie!" someone calls. I look up to my main tormentor, Eddie Halvorsen. Eddie is a short, wiry senior boy in a greasy cap and faded camo duck jacket; I heard he used to play soccer all the time and wanted to be in the Olympics but then his knees gave out. Something genetic, they said. Eddie grins at me. Mountain Dew drips down my cheek and across my lips; I had forgotten that Mountain Dew was so sweet.

"Hey, pick up my can, Weird Suzy," Eddie says. I bend down to get it. I place it carefully in my garbage bag. Everyone cheers.

"This too, freak," Eddie says. He steps closer; he has a limp. From between his thumb and middle finger he flips his cigarette directly at me. I'm not quick enough to avoid it, but would not have anyway. The cigarette stings my cheek like a bee. Sparks fly as the butt falls at my feet. I touch my cheek; gray ash comes off on my finger tip.

"Hey! Halvorsen!" an adult voice calls sharply. "I saw that."

I draw my ashy finger slowly across my forehead, then bend to pick up the dead butt.

The parking lot monitor, an off-duty security guard, trots across the street. He comes first to me.

"Are you all right, miss?" he says.

"I'm fine," I say softly.

"You could have put her eye out," the guard says, catching Eddie by the arm.

Eddie shrugs. "I was just getting rid of my butt. Can't help it if she got in the way."

"If this were on school property, you'd be gone—for good," the guard says.

"But it ain't. It's public property. I got my rights, now shove off and stop bothering me."

After speaking into his little radio, the guard crosses the street back to school property. There he stands with his arms crossed and glares at Eddie.

"Way to go, Eddie. Cool, man!" his friends call. Eddie grins. His teeth have gone bad from Mountain Dew and chewing tobacco.

Then the first hour bell rings.

My tormenters look at one another, then swear loudly. They slam the contents of pop bottles down their throats and take last draws on their cigarettes. Burping and cursing, they throw down their trash, then trudge onto school property. I wait for them to leave. My cheek stings a little but I keep working with my garbage bag.

"Suzanne—come along now," a voice says.

I look up. It's the assistant principal, Ms. Kaufman.

"I'm almost done," I say.

"You *are* done, Suzanne. Come along," she says firmly. She takes my garbage bag in one hand and my arm in the other. She reminds me of my real mother, who is in prison. I have not told anyone in River Forks about this. Only my aunt and I know. My aunt thinks it's best that way. Sometimes I'm not so sure.

"Remember, Suzanne, you have the counselor this morning, then regular classes after that."

I nod.

"Tell me your schedule today?" she says. Her voice is closer now; she has leaned in to stare at my cheek.

"Counselor. Then my regular classes." I recite my schedule. Often people think I'm not listening to them. But I hear everything.

"That's right," she says. "But first you 'd better drop by the nurse's office and get your face looked at. There's a little blister on your cheek."

"Eddie," I say. I touch the burned spot.

"The parking lot monitor told me. Would you like to fill out a harassment report?"

WWJD? "No," I say.

"I really encourage you to do so. Eddie is out of control these days. You would be helping him."

"A change of heart must come from the inside," I murmur. I turn left toward the nurse's office. Behind me

Mrs. Kaufman sighs. I can feel her standing there, watching me. She waits, I suppose, to make sure I actually go see the nurse. I can feel her eyes pushing on my back.

Ms. Jones, the nurse, puts ointment on my face. She tries to wipe clean the ash mark but I lean away. "I consider it a religious symbol," I say.

"Excuse me?" she says. She is quite young, and possibly has no religion. Most people don't these days, especially in public schools.

"Like the mark Catholics wear on Ash Wednesday," I add.

"Suzanne, today is Monday."

"Religious markings are protected under the Constitution," I say. This is enough to make her lower the moist towelette.

Her eyes flicker down the rest of me. At my hair. At my clothes, which I get from the Salvation Army. At my sandals, which I made myself in shop class from tire rubber, leather straps, and buckles. At my long orange scarf, which I wear everywhere. Her eyes return to my hair.

"Are you keeping up your hygiene, Suzanne?" she says. "Good personal hygiene is important—particularly for girls." She smiles and winks.

"I'm fine," I say.

"Let me give you some samples of shampoo and deodorant," she says. "I get them free. I want you to try them and let me know how you like them. Some of them smell *so* nice."

"Thank you, Ms. Jones," I say, and take the white plastic bag. It is one of dozens from a large box labeled STUDENT HYGIENE KITS.

We look at each other. She blinks first.

"Okay, you may go, Suzanne," she says.

"Thank you," I say.

"Be sure to drop by and let me know which shampoo you liked best," she adds.

Next I go to the counselor's office. "Suzanne," the secretary says cheerfully.

I smile. I'm a regular here. They have a school program for new and transfer students called "Meeters and Greeters." For a while I met with a boy and girl my own age, but gradually they were replaced by adults. I'm not sure why. As I wait, I hear loud voices behind the door. Then Eddie Halvorsen emerges from Mr. Klephorn's office. He is red-faced, and glares at me as he passes. "Crazy freak," he grunts. "Now you're really on my list."

I only stare at him and smile.

"Who's next? Why, it's Suzanne!" Mr. Klephorn calls heartily. His face is flushed from talking with Eddie. "Come on in!" A hearty greeting is requisite for all counselors. That and positive body language. Inside his office he sits beside me in one of the comfortable chairs; he keeps his knees open, his arms unfolded. He does not stay behind his desk like some counselors.

"Suzanne, how are things?" he begins. He has a nice smile.

"Fine," I say. I smile back.

He glances at a memo on his desk. "I understand that you had an encounter with Eddie Halvorsen this morning."

"Nothing serious."

"That's not what the parking lot monitor said."

"Really, it was nothing."

"Well, I've just spoken to Eddie," he says.

"There was no need. I have no complaint against Eddie. I think he's going through tough times right now. Jesus is trying to speak to him."

Mr. Klephorn purses his lips. "He burned your cheek. I can see the mark from here."

"And I've forgiven him."

"Suzanne, we've talked about this . . . forgiveness thing."

"Yes," I say.

"I know you're a very religious person," he continues. I nod.

"You read the Bible every day."

"Yes. Though mainly in the New Testament. I find the Old Testament too centered upon retribution, revenge. Jesus believed not in punishment but in forgiveness. In turning the other cheek."

"Yes, of course, Suzanne," he says quickly. "But my point, one we've talked about before, is that this is the twenty-first century. These are different times than when Jesus lived. And we must live in them. We must inhabit our *own* times, so to speak."

I wait.

He clears his throat. "While Jesus provided us wonderful lessons, it is, may I say, perhaps unrealistic to try and live His example every minute of our day."

There is silence as I think about that. Then I say, "But isn't that why we go to church? Why we read the Bible? To live more like Jesus?"

He leans back, appears to consider that. Most counselors only pretend to think about what you say, but Mr. Klephorn seems to actually listen sometimes. "Yes, you're right, Suzanne," he says at length. "But within limits. That's my point here—within limits."

"There are no limits to forgiveness," I say.

Mr. Klephorn stares, then checks his wristwatch. "Otherwise, things are good, Suzanne?" he says. His voice is louder and heartier again; this is a signal that we are done.

"Fine," I say.

"How are things at home?"

"Good."

"Your aunt . . ."

"Jean."

"Thank you. Aunt Jean is around full time?"

"Yes," I say. I do not tell him that she works the night shift at the truck stop, and is usually asleep when I get home. But she's very good about bringing home food—especially day-old desserts—and leaving it out for me. I usually have pie several times a day.

"Good." He pauses. His eyes drop to my clothes, to my long bright scarf. "One more thing. Remember our dress code at RFH, Suzanne. It's probably different than California. Here you may of course choose your own clothes, but they mustn't be disruptive or extreme. Page four, section 3-c of the Student Council Handbook."

"Thank you, Mr. Klephorn," I say. We shake hands.

My day goes all right. For lunch I get a milk to go along with my piece of restaurant pie. In the cafeteria I sit by myself as usual. I see some of the Meeters and Greeters kids from earlier in the year, but they are all sitting together. I don't mind. What I'm looking forward to is my last class of the day, woodworking. I've always liked to make things, plus I don't mind being surrounded by boys (I'm the only girl). It is among boys that I can do the most good.

At 2:00 P.M. I go to woodworking. Eddie Halvorsen is there, along with the other "woodies," as they call themselves. He glares at me.

"Safety glasses," Mr. Patterson says automatically.

Eddie mutters something at me as I pass by to my shop locker. There I spin my combination padlock and take out my wooden swan lamp. I touch its long dark neck.

One of Eddie's friends eases up to me. "You sign?" he asks, meaning did I sign a harassment complaint.

"No," I say.

"Why not?

"I forgive him."

"You're beyond weird." He oozes away, whispers to Eddie, who glares at me, then spits out words that even I can hear above the start-up hum of the machines. His friends look at him oddly.

I begin work on my wooden swan. I use a hand-held sanding block. I don't like machines; they're too loud, and can cut too quickly into the wood. I like to go slow. The neck of my black walnut swan curves up gracefully. I've been working on her all term, and she's really getting beautiful. Even Mr. Patterson complimented me on her. He let me do a project different from the boys, most of whom are making gun cabinets. But I love my swan. When I work on her, she reminds me that there is hope for Eddie. For all of us. My swan started as a rough piece of black walnut—hard and full of splinters. First I cut her outline with a band saw, then used a power sander for one day to round her neck and breast. Now each day she gets smoother. The grain of the wood is beginning to come out. It looks almost like tiny feathers.

After school, on my way home, it is snowing. I walk with my head down and my scarf wrapped around my face. It never snowed in California. Suddenly someone blocks the sidewalk. "Weird Suzy!" Eddie says.

I stop. Blink.

He has popped out of the alley; deeper in it, by a sagging garage, a group of his friends are looking at something in a small bag.

"Hello, Eddie," I say. For a moment he scares me. But I remember that Jesus must have been afraid many times.

"How's come you didn't sign?" he says. His eyes, small and very dark—like knots in black walnut—bore into mine.

"I don't believe in retaliation," I say.

"Turn the other cheek, that kind of bull?"

I nod.

He laughs hoarsely. "If you'da signed, I'd be kicked out of school for good. Then I wouldn't be around to bother you."

"Where would you go, what would you do out of school?" I answer.

He stares. There is a pause. By then the others in the alley are looking at us. Suddenly Eddie whoops and snakes out his arm; he grabs my orange scarf and strips it from my neck.

"Hey everybody!" he shouts. He wraps it around his neck and dances just out of my reach.

I blink against the falling snow and look at him. WWJD? I set down my book bag, take off my coat, hold it out to him. "Take my coat too," I say.

He stops, stares. Then he grabs my coat, throws it in the snow.

"My hat too," I say. I take off my beret, hand it to him. He throws it in the snow. He laughs.

I peel off my sweater—I have on only a T-shirt underneath and it is suddenly very chilly—and I hand it to him. After a moment's hesitation, he takes it.

"Hey, Eddie, no!" one of his friends says.

"You're gonna get us in trouble, Eddie," another calls.

"She's crazy, Eddie. Don't!"

The kids in the alley scatter. Now there is only Eddie and me. He swallows as he stares at me. I am shivering in the February air. Suddenly he flings my sweater in my face so hard I stumble back. "What in hell is the matter with you?" he says. His voice cracks. When I look up again, he is limping quickly away, disappearing in the snow after his friends.

The next morning I walk to school the usual way. Eddie's gang spots me, as usual. "Hey, Eddie, it's Weird Suzy," someone calls.

But this morning Eddie will not look at me. He stands with his back to me, his hands jammed in his pockets. I can feel his anger. His hard heart. Light snow is falling again and has whitened his cap and shoulders. For a moment he looks like a pillar of salt.

In shop class Eddie's dark eyes follow me as I go to my locker, unlock it, carefully take out my swan lamp. I go to my station and begin work. Working on my swan makes me forget everything, even my mother. Later this week Mr. Patterson will help me drill the hole for the cord and the lightbulb post. Then I'll be ready for the final sanding and varnishing. I stroke my swan's dark neck. Parts of it are smoother than human skin.

"What the hell's that supposed to be, anyway?" Eddie says in my ear. I turn. He grabs at my swan. I jerk it away from him and cradle it in my arms. Mr. Patterson is on the far side of the shop helping someone with the table saw. He can't help me. Eddie laughs.

I feel my face flush. I shouldn't have jerked my swan away from Eddie. It's not something Jesus would have done. Slowly I hold it out so that he can see it—but not touch it.

"It's a swan," I say.

"Looks like a damned crow to me," Eddie says.

"It's not finished," I answer. "Like all of us."

He stares at me. I see the hate in his eyes.

"You should have stayed in California, you freak."

After he leaves I turn back to my swan but my hands are shaky. For one brief moment I understand what Jesus felt like when He knew that He was the One. The Chosen One. "Take this cup," I murmur to my swan. "Choose someone else to help Eddie." But she is silent.

I do not see Eddie after school, which today is all right by me. The weather has cleared—there is low red sunlight on fresh snow—and I take a walk down by the river. The Fork River runs through town, and in winter it is good for skiing and skating upon. It still is amazing to me that people can walk on water. This winter, however, spring has come early; posted along the bank are "Danger—Thin Ice!" signs.

I like the river. It's quieter here, and there are little benches to sit on. One place I think of as my own. I often come down here to pray. Today I pray for my mother— that she will not forget me—and especially for Eddie Halvorsen. I feel like he is close to a breakthrough. I pray for a long time, until I'm cold and have to go home.

Near school the next morning Eddie calls out to me. "Hey, Suzy! How's it going?"

I stare. His voice is almost cheerful. None of his friends throw anything at me. They are all smiling. I do not quite understand this, but not everything Jesus does is understandable. I smile a little, nod and pass by.

It is a good day at school. People seem pleased to see me, even the college prep crowd. In California it was lowriders, Chicanos, valley girls; here it's the jocks, the farmers, the motorheads. Everybody looks at me as I pass by. I guess I'm my own crowd. Still, today everyone seems extra friendly.

In shop class I go straight to my locker. I can't wait to get started. But my padlock, broken, falls into my hands. I stare at it, then at my little metal door. Its hinges are bent. Slowly I pull open the door. My swan falls out in pieces. She clatters to the floor like a spilled puzzle that cannot ever be put right. I can't help myself: I drop to my knees, clutch the pieces, and begin to wail. I hear myself calling for my mother.

* * *

I leave school late. I have been in the nurse's office. "Eddie won't be back in school. Not after this," the nurse says. I can't think of anything to say. Finally she lets me go home.

Outside, all the yellow buses are gone. The snow has stopped and it is colder again. The sun is low and orange and will be setting soon.

I head down by the river, when I am aware of footsteps.

"Hey, Weird Suzy," Eddie says. "What happened to your crow?"

I stop. "It was a swan," I blurt. "A black swan." There is laughter from his gang, which is smaller now—only three besides Eddie.

I hunch under my scarf and keep walking.

"You see what happened when you didn't sign that form? You should have gotten rid of me when you could," Eddie says, limping after me.

I keep walking.

"So where you going now, Weird Suzy?" he says.

"Down by the river," I say.

"Gonna drown yourself?" Eddie says. He laughs with an odd, high-pitched sound. His friends chuckle uncertainly.

"Maybe today's the day," he whispers, close behind me now.

"Hey, Eddie, don't," someone says.

"If not now, when, Weird Suzy?" Eddie says, his breath strong and sweet from chewing tobacco.

"Come on, Eddie, let's go, man." The others have dropped back a little. But not Eddie.

To get away, I head down the bank, past a "Danger— Thin Ice!" sign.

"That's right. Good girl!" Eddie calls. He follows me down the bank.

I step onto the ice. Wind has blown it bare in spots. There are tiny bubbles trapped in its glass. The frozen bubbles show me how thick the ice is. I walk out several yards.

"For God's sake, Eddie!" his friends call. They retreat to the parkway, as if they are safe there.

I walk farther out, toward the middle of the river where there is a dark, steaming, open patch. I think of Jesus when He walked on water. It was all a matter of faith.

I move a couple of steps closer to the black water. Then I turn and face Eddie, who remains on the white shore. "Are you coming?" I say. "Don't be afraid."

He laughs but there is something thin and reedy and strangled in his throat.

"You can do it," I say. I beckon him forward.

He glances up toward the parkway; his friends stare down at him.

"You're crazy," he says. He steps onto the ice. Though he is heavier than me, it holds him just fine. He comes closer.

"Come out to where I am," I say.

He stops.

"It's all a matter of not being afraid," I say.

He takes several more steps—and suddenly there is a sound under his feet like foil ripping. Eddie's arms flap, like a bird taking off, as his legs and trunk disappear through the ice. He screams. I wonder if my black swan screamed when its head was cut off.

"Oh, shit!" someone shouts from the bank.

Suddenly, Eddie is hanging on to the ice by his elbows. Most of his body is underwater.

"Help!" he shouts to his friends. "Help me!"

They run away. Perhaps to get help, perhaps just to run. A car stops on the parkway; the driver quickly lifts a cell phone to his face.

"Save me," Eddie screams. "Someone! Suzy! Please! Save me!"

I watch him. I think of my swan. My butchered black swan. I think, What would Jesus do? Possibly I could save Eddie, though he seems to have a grip on the ice. I have my long orange scarf. It would be enough to throw to him. It would be something for him to hold on to until help arrives. But I understand that not even Jesus could save everyone.

I sit down on the ice just out of Eddie's reach. I must think about what to do. After all, I am only human.

Will Weaver

Before writing for teens, Will Weaver published two books for adults: *A Gravestone Made of Wheat* and *Red Earth, White Earth*. His first young adult novel, *Striking Out*, was a hit with readers as well as with critics, and it was named a Best Book for Young Adults by the American Library Association. That novel introduced readers to Billy Baggs, a thirteen-year-old farm boy who discovers he has talent as a baseball pitcher. Baseball provides him with a diversion from the harsh life of the farm, which includes a demanding father.

The growing pleasure Billy finds in playing baseball continues in *Farm Team* (an ALA Best Book for Young Adults), although his father is in jail and Billy and his mother must take care of the farm. For fun, they organize a motley baseball team in order to challenge the town team.

When Billy heads for high school in *Hard Ball* (third in the series and also an ALA Best Book), his biggest problems come in the form of the most beautiful girl in ninth grade and an ongoing rivalry with "King" Kenwood, an ace pitcher as well as a rich townie.

Will Weaver, who grew up on a Minnesota farm, now lives in Bemidji, Minnesota, and teaches creative writing at Bemidji State University. He says the idea for "WWJD" began with the phrase itself. "It interested me because it's a concept nearly impossible to live up to," he explains. "As well, religion, teenagers, and school always make an uneasy threesome. The potential for conflict is very high, and for a writer, conflict is story."

Weaver's newest novel is called *Memory Boy,* a story set in the near future, focusing on a suburban family who has to leave the city and pull together in order to survive a world-class ecological disaster.

Satyagraha

Alden R. Carter

The kid from India seems to be a pretty nice guy, even though he talks a little funny. But he doesn't have a clue how to survive in an American high school, especially when an all-conference defensive end starts bashing him against the lockers.

RAMDAS BAHAVE MET me at the sidelines. "In what part of the body are you wounded, Kenneth?" he asked.

"Hand," I gritted.

"The smallest finger again?"

"Yeah."

"Let me see it, please."

I held out my right hand, the dislocated little finger already twice normal size and rapidly turning purple.

Rollin Acres, my best buddy and the team's fullback, made a barfing sound. "Jeez, I wish you'd stop messing up that finger, Ken. It's disgusting."

"Just watch the game, Rollin."

"Sure. But, you know, if you had a little more vertical you could catch a pass like that."

"I've got more vertical than you do, jerk."

"You're supposed to. You're a tight end. Who ever heard of a fullback with vertical leap?"

Ramdas interrupted. "Would you like me to correct this problem now?"

"Yeah, do it," I said.

Ramdas took my pinkie in his strong, slender fingers and pulled. Pain shot up my arm and my eyes teared. Dang! This time he really was going to pull it out by the roots. Then there was a pop and sudden easing of the pain. He felt gently along the joint. "It is back in place. Are you all right? Feel faint, perhaps?"

"I'm okay. Just tape me up and get me back in."

He made a disapproving sound but started buddy-taping my pinkie and ring fingers. Out on the field we'd covered the punt and held Gentry High to four yards on two running plays. Still time to win if we could hold them on third down. "Come on, Patch," I yelled. "Now's the time."

"Please hold your hand still, Kenneth," Ramdas said.

The Gentry quarterback dropped back to pass as Bill Patchett, our all-conference defensive end, bull-rushed their left tackle. Bill slung the kid aside, leaped a shot at his ankles by the fullback, and buried the quarterback. The ball popped loose and Bill dove on it, but the ref signaled no fumble, down by contact. Bill jumped up and started yelling at the ref, but a couple of the other seniors pulled him away before he got a flag.

Ramdas handed me a bag of ice. "Here. Sit down. Rest."

"I can't sit down. We're getting the ball back."

While Gentry set up to punt, Coach Carlson strolled down the line to me. "Finger again?"

"Yes, sir."

"Can you play?"

"Yes, sir."

Coach looked at Ramdas, who shrugged. "It is a dislocation like the other times. I think he should keep ice on it."

Coach looked at me. "Right hand?"

I nodded.

"Hard for you to hold on to a football, then. I'll put in Masanz."

So that was it for me for that game. We got the ball back on our thirty with two minutes to go. Marvin Katt, our quarterback, got two quick completions against their prevent defense but couldn't connect on the big pass downfield. Final score: 16–10. Yet another loss for ol' Argyle High.

Bill Patchett spent his usual five minutes bashing his fists, forearms, and head into lockers. At six four, 240, that's a lot of frustration on the loose, and the rest of us stayed out of his way. "Hey, Bauer," he yelled at me. "Where were you on that last series?"

I held up my bandaged hand. "Dislocated a finger."

"And so little doc Ramdas wouldn't let you play, huh?"

"It wasn't like that, Bill."

He didn't listen. Instead he grabbed a roll of tape and fired it at Ramdas, who was straightening up the training room, his back to us. The roll of tape flew through the open door and did a three-cushion bank shot around the room. Ramdas jumped out of the way and looked at us in confusion.

"Hey, Ramboy!" Bill yelled. "Your job is to get people back in, not keep them out!"

Ramdas didn't answer, only stared. That just made Bill madder, and he started for the door, fists balled. "The idea is to win, you jerk! No matter what it costs. So unless a guy's got an arm ripped off, you get him back in!"

Rollin stepped in front of him. "Come on, Bill. We all feel like crap about losing. You played—"

"He doesn't feel like crap! He doesn't care one way or the other as long as he gets to play with his bandages and his ice packs."

"Yeah, yeah, sure, Bill," Rollin said. "Just let it alone now. Go take a shower. You'll feel better."

Bill stalked back to his corner, smashed another locker door, and started pulling off his uniform.

I got into the passenger seat of the Toyota pickup piloted by my liberated, noncommitted, female friend, Sarah Landwehr. (You can call her my girlfriend if you've got the guts. I don't.) "Tough loss," Sarah said.

"Aren't they all? A couple more, and we'll have to start replacing lockers."

"Billy Patch took it out on poor, defenseless inanimate objects again, huh?"

"Yep. He got after Ramdas too. Rollin broke it up."

"What's with Bill, anyway? It's not Ramdas's fault you guys lost."

"Well, Ramdas would rather sit a guy down than risk making an injury worse. Bill doesn't think that's the way to win football games."

Sarah snorted. "So he thinks you should risk permanent injury just to win a stupid game?"

"Something like that. Let's go to Mac's. I'm hungry." I started fiddling with the radio dial, hoping she'd let the subject drop.

She didn't, which is pretty typical of her. "I still don't get it. There's got to be more to it than that."

I sighed. How to explain? "Ramdas doesn't seem to care if we win or lose. And that drives Bill nuts. I mean, look at it from his standpoint. Here he is, the best player on a lousy team. He's been all-conference, but he could have been all-state if he'd played in a winning program. And all-state means a scholarship and the chance to play for a Division One or a Division Two school. All-conference doesn't guarantee anything."

"None of that justifies being mean to Ramdas."

"No, but it explains it a little."

She harrumphed, unimpressed. "So what's going to happen next? Is Bill going to start punching him?"

"I don't think it'll come to that."

"Well, I think it might! And I think you'd better do something about it, *team captain*."

"Only one of four."

"Still—"

"I know, I know. I'll keep an eye on things."

She glared at me. "You should do a heck of a lot more than that, Kenny."

Maybe she was right, but I didn't plan on doing anything. If Ramdas felt there was a big problem, he should go to Coach Carlson. Me, I was going to ignore the whole thing as long as possible.

We didn't have practice Monday, and I didn't see anything of Ramdas or Bill until Tuesday morning. Rollin and I were coming down the east corridor maybe twenty feet behind Bill when Ramdas turned the corner. Bill took a step to his left and put a shoulder into him. Ramdas bounced off the lockers, skidded on the slippery floor, and only just managed to keep his balance. Bill didn't even look back.

"Oh-oh," I said. "I hope Bill doesn't make a habit of that."

"He already has," Rollin said. "Started yesterday morning. Every time he sees Ramdas, *wham*, into the lockers."

"Wow, did you say anything to him?"

"To Bill?"

"Yeah."

"I said something. Asked him why. He says he's gonna get Ramdas's attention one way or another."

"I don't think getting his attention is the problem."

"Neither do I, but are you going to argue with someone as big and ornery as Billy Patch?"

No, and it wouldn't do any good if I did. Besides, I had a couple questions of my own for Ramdas.

At noon I found him sitting by himself in the cafeteria, a textbook open beside his tray. I sat down across from him. "Hey, Ram," I said.

"Hello, Kenneth." He marked his place, closed the book, and looked at me expectantly.

"Why do you always use people's full names?"

He smiled, shrugged slightly. "I like their sound. I do not like to use contractions either. I like the full words."

"It makes you sound like a professor or something."

"Sorry."

"Uh, well, not a problem. But, look, you've got to do something about this thing between you and Bill Patchett."

"What would you suggest?"

"For starters you could act like you care if the team wins or loses."

"But I do not care. Football is a lot of pointless violence as far as I can see."

"Then why'd you volunteer to be a trainer?"

"To help with the wounded."

I shook my head. "Well, maybe you could at least stop being so passive about everything."

He laughed. "You would have me fight William Patchett?"

"Well, not exactly, but—"

"Because I will not fight. It goes against everything I believe."

"I don't expect you to fight him, but you can stand up to him in other ways."

"But I am."

"How's that?"

"By not reacting with force. Force is never justified."

"Well, maybe not in this case, but—"

"No, Kenneth, in all cases. Never, no matter how good the cause."

"Oh, come on. How else are we supposed to keep other people or other countries from taking what's ours? Sometimes you've got to use force."

He sighed. "I guess that is what a lot of you Americans believe. But I believe that you can resist in another way. Mahatma Gandhi called it *satyagraha*, to stand firmly for truth and love without ever resorting to force."

I stared at him in disbelief. I mean, Bill was about to turn him into a smear of jelly and Ramdas was talking about some dead holy man! "Well, that may be very cool, Ram, but—"

"You have heard of Gandhi, have you not?"

"Sure. I mean, the name, anyway. And I'd love to hear more. But right now I think you'd better tell me what you're planning to do about Bill Patchett."

"I am telling you. The Mahatma used *satyagraha* to free all of India from the British. I think I can use it to control Mr. William Patchett."

Oh, sure. But I bet Gandhi never had to face down six foot four, 240 pounds of crazed defensive end. "Ram, listen—"

He interrupted gently. "Let me tell you a story. Under British rule it was illegal for Indians to make their own salt. Everyone had to buy expensive government salt, and that was very hard on the poor. Three thousand of the Mahatma's followers went to protest the law at a place called the Dharasana Salt Works. They stepped four at a time up to a line of soldiers, never lifting a hand to defend themselves, and let the soldiers beat them down with bamboo clubs. Those who could got up and went to the back of the line. All day they marched up to the soldiers until the soldiers were so tired they could not lift their arms."

"What did that prove?"

"It proved that the Mahatma's followers were willing to suffer for what they believed without doing hurt to others. Their example brought hundreds of thousands of new recruits to the struggle for independence. Eventually, the jails were full and the country did not work anymore and the British had to leave."

It was my turn to sigh, because this had gotten a long way from football or figuring out a way to keep Bill from turning Ramdas into an ooze of pink on a locker door. "Look, Ramdas, that might have worked in India, but in this country—"

"Your Martin Luther King made it work in this country."

"Okay, point taken, but what are you going to do about Bill?"

"Just what I am doing. I am going to answer his violence with *satyagraha*. Someday, his arms will get tired."

"If he doesn't kill you first."

Ramdas smiled faintly. "There is always a risk."

Ramdas didn't get it. OK, he was Indian, had moved here with his family only a couple of years ago. But somehow he must have gotten this *satyagraha* thing wrong. No way could it work. During study hall I went to the library, figuring I could find something that would prove it to him. All the Internet computers were busy, so I went to the shelves. I found a thick book with a lot of photographs of Gandhi and sat down to page through it. And . . . it . . . blew . . . me . . . away. Here was this skinny little guy with thick glasses and big ears wandering around in sandals and a loincloth, and he'd won! And I mean big time: freed his country without ever lifting his hand against anybody. Incredible.

Now, I'm not the kind who tosses and turns half the night worrying about things. I'm a jock. I need my sleep.

When I hit the pillow, bam, I'm gone. But that night I lay thinking until well past midnight. Hadn't Jesus said to turn the other cheek? Ramdas was living that, and he was a Hindu or something, while most of the guys I saw in church on Sunday would prefer to beat the other guy to a pulp. Man, oh, man, I didn't need this. Let Sarah and Ramdas talk philosophy; I was just a jock. But like it or not, I was going to have to do something or feel like a hypocrite forever.

Wednesday morning I went to see Coach Carlson with my plan. He didn't like it. "Look, I'll get Patchett's attention," he said. "I'll tell him to quit giving Ramdas a hard time."

"Coach, I really want to do this. For a lot of reasons."

We talked some more and he finally agreed, though he still didn't like it much.

Next I talked to Rollin. He shook his head. "Man, you could get hurt. And I mean *bad*."

"I'll take that chance. Just tell the other guys not to step in. And if Ramdas starts, you stop him."

Finally, I told Sarah. She studied me for a long minute. "You're not really doing this for Ramdas, are you?"

"I'm not sure."

"Can I shoot Bill with a tranquilizer dart if things get out of hand?"

"I guess that wouldn't be too bad an idea. But I don't think they will. He's big, but I'm pretty big too."

Bill Patchett takes everything seriously, which makes it all the scarier practicing against him. Bill is, by the way, not a moron. He maintains a 4.0 in a full load of honors classes and is the only kid in school with the guts to carry a briefcase. On the football field, he studies an opponent, figures out his moves, and then pancakes him or blows by him. Believe me, I know; I've been practicing against him for years. But as I'd reminded Sarah, I'm big too, and I'd seen all his moves.

We lined up for pass rushing/blocking drill. The center hiked the ball to Marvin Katt, who was back in the shotgun. Billy Patch hit me with a straight bull rush. I took it, letting him run over me. When I got up and took my stance for the next play, he gave me a funny look. "Ready this time?"

"Yep," I said, and set my feet to make it just as hard as possible for him.

Cat Man yelled, "Hut, Hut, HUT!" and there was the familiar crash of helmets and shoulder pads. Bill hit me so hard my teeth rattled. Every instinct told me to bring up my arms to defend myself, but I just took the hit. I landed flat on my back, the air whooshing out of my lungs.

He glared down at me. "C'mon, Bauer. Get with the program, huh?"

He must have figured I was trying to sucker him, because the third time he took a step to the right, as if he expected me to come at him hard. Instead, I took a step to my left to get in front of him and let him run me down.

After that play he didn't talk and he didn't try to go around me. He just came at me as hard as he could. After a while the other players stopped practicing and just watched. Cat Man would yell, "Hut, Hut, HUT!" and the same thing would happen again. I lost count how many times Bill decked me. Finally, he hit me so hard my ears rang and the back of my helmet bounced two or three times on the turf. I just lay there, almost too stunned to move, as he stalked off toward the locker room. But it wasn't quite enough. Not yet.

Somehow I managed to stumble to my feet. "Hey, Bill! I can still stand, Bill. Can still stand up to you." He turned and came at me with a roar. And it was the hardest thing I'd ever done in my life to take that hit without trying to protect myself. He hit me with every ounce of his 240, drove me into the turf, and the world flashed black and then back to light.

We lay a yard apart, panting. "Okay," he gasped. "I give up. What's this all about?"

"It's about standing up without fighting back."

"Don't give me puzzles, man. I'm too tired."

"It's about Ramdas. He doesn't want to fight."

"The little weasel should stand up for himself."

"He is, just like I did now. He calls it *satyagraha*. I don't know if I'm even pronouncing it right, but it means standing firm without using force. He won't fight no matter what you do."

"That's dumb."

"It's what he believes. I think he's got a right to that."

We sat up, still breathing hard. Bill took off his helmet and wiped sweat from his face. "You were driving me crazy. This was harder than a game. I'm whipped."

I took a breath. "Ramdas told me a story." I told him about the three thousand guys who'd walked up to the soldiers at the Dharasana Salt Works and let themselves get beaten down with clubs.

Bill listened. "And that worked, huh?"

"Yeah, it did."

He shook his head. "I couldn't do that. I don't have the guts." He struggled to his feet and plodded toward the sidelines where Sarah, Ramdas, Coach Carlson, and most of the team were watching. Passing Ramdas, he laid a hand briefly on his shoulder. It wasn't much, but a start maybe.

Ramdas met me halfway to the sideline. "In what part of the body are you wounded this time, Kenneth?"

"All over, but nothing special."

"Your hand. It is all right?"

"Fine."

He hesitated. "And your spirit? How is it?"

I looked at him, saw his eyes shining with something that might have been laughter or maybe a joy I didn't quite understand but thought I recognized from the old black-and-white pictures of Gandhi and his followers.

"Feeling not too bad," I said. "Not bad at all."

Alden R. Carter

Before becoming a writer, Alden Carter was an officer in the United States Navy and a high school English teacher. In the twenty years he has been a full-time writer, Carter has published five picture books for and about children with special needs, twenty nonfiction books, and nine highly praised novels for teenagers. Among those novels are *Sheila's Dying*, *Up Country*, *Dogwolf*, and *Between a Rock and a Hard Place*.

Up Country was named by the American Library Association as one of the 100 Best of the Best Books for Young Adults published between 1967 and 1992. His more recent novel *Bull Catcher*—a story about the friendship between two high school baseball players—was named one of the Ten Best Books for Young Adults of 1997 by the ALA and won the prestigious Heartland Award for Excellence in Young Adult Literature.

Carter's most recent novel, *Crescent Moon*, a historical novel set in northern Wisconsin in the early 1900's, grew out of the lively stories his father told about the lumber industry. Shortly after publication, the novel was named to the New York Public Library's Books for the Teen Age list.

While discussing plot possibilities for this short story, Carter was reminded of a very talented Indian boy he had once taught in a workshop. "I suspect that many American teenage readers will view Ramdas's tactics with great skepticism," the author says. "But Gandhi proved that *satyagraha* can work and today hundreds of millions of people worldwide live by his example. It's worth our giving some thought to it."

You can learn more about author Alden R. Carter and his numerous fiction and nonfiction books by logging onto his website at www.tznet.com/busn/acarterwriter.

A Letter from the Fringe

Joan Bauer

Every kid at the fringe table has been a victim of cruel remarks from the "in crowd," and Dana, who has been their target too often, wants to change things. But does she have the courage to tell the kids in school how they've made her and her friends feel? And will telling them make any difference?

TODAY THEY GOT SALLY.

She wasn't doing anything. Just eating a cookie that her aunt had made for her. It was a serious cookie too. She'd given me one. It was still in my mouth with the white chocolate and pecans and caramel all swirling together.

I saw Doug Booker before she did.

Saw his eyes get that hard glint they always get right before he says something mean. Watched him walk toward us squeezing his hands into fists, getting psyched for the match. He's a champion varsity wrestler known for overwhelming his opponents in the first round. He was joined by Charlie Bass, brute ice hockey goalie, who was smirking and laughing and looking at Sally like the mere sight of her hurt his eyes.

Get the Geeks is a popular bonding ritual among the jock flock at Bronley High.

I swallowed my cookie. Felt my stomach tense. It was too late to grab Sally and walk off.

"Fun company at four o'clock," I warned her.

Sally looked up to smirks. Her face went pale.

Booker did that vibrato thing with his voice that he thinks is so funny. "So, *Sals,* maybe you should be cutting back on those calories, huh?"

Charlie was laughing away.

"What have you got, Sals, about thirty pounds to lose? More?" He did a *tsk, tsk.* Looked her up and down with premium disgust.

All she could do was look down.

I stood up. "Get lost, Booker."

Sneer. Snort. "Now, how can I get lost in school?"

"Booker, I think you have the innate ability to get lost just about anywhere."

"Why don't you and your fat friend just get out of my face because the two of you are so butt ugly you're making me sick and I don't know if I can hold the puke in!"

He and Charlie strolled off.

There's no response to that kind of hate.

I looked at Sally, who was gripping her cookie bag.

I tried fighting through the words like my mom and dad had taught me. Taking each one apart like I'm diffusing a bomb.

Was Sally fat?

I sucked in my stomach. She needed to lose some weight, but who doesn't?

Were she and I so disgusting we could make someone sick?

We're not Hollywood starlets, if that's his measuring stick.

If Booker said we were serial killers, we could have shrugged it off. But gifted bullies use partial truths. Doug knew how to march into personal territory.

I didn't know what to say. I blustered out, "They're total creeps, Sally."

No response.

"I mean, you've got a right to eat a cookie without getting hassled. You know those guys love hurting people. They think they've got some inalienable privilege—"

A tear rolled down her cheek. "I do have to lose weight, Dana."

"They don't have a right to say it! There are all kinds of sizes in this world that are perfectly fine!"

She sat there broken, holding the cookie bag that I just noticed had pictures of balloons on it.

"It's my birthday," she said quietly.

"Oh, Sally, I didn't know that."

Sally and I were at the fringe table in the back of the lunchroom. It was as far away from the in-crowd table as you could get and still be in the cafeteria. The best thing about the fringe table is that everyone who sits at it is bonded together by the strands of social victimization. We all just deal with it differently.

Present were:

Cedric Melville, arch techno whiz, hugely tall with wild-man hair and a beak nose. He has an unusual habit of standing on one leg like a flamingo. Booker calls him "Maggot."

Jewel Lardner, zany artist with pink-striped hair who has spent years studying the systems of the ICIs. ICIs are In-Crowd Individuals. She'd long ago stopped caring about being in, out, or in between.

Gil Mishkin, whose car got covered with shaving cream last week in the parking lot. Gil doesn't have much hair because of a skin condition. His head has round, hairless patches and most of his eyebrows are gone. He can't shave and is embarrassed about it. Booker calls him "Bald Boy."

"Now, with big, popular Doug," Cedric said, "you can't give him much room to move, which is what you did. When you shot right back at him, he came back harder. He always does that."

"He'll do something else, though," said Gil. "Remember what happened to my car." His hand went self-consciously over his half-bald head.

"Look," said Jewel, "you're talking defensive moves here. You've got to think offensively so the ICIs leave you alone. First off, you guys need cell phones. That way, if any of us sees big trouble coming, we can warn the others. If a jock on the prowl comes close to me, I whip out my phone and start shouting into it, 'Are you kidding me? He's got *what* kind of disease? Is it catching?' People don't come near you when you're talking disease."

"But most important," said Ed Looper, plunking his lunch tray down, "is you can't seem like a victim."

"I don't seem like a victim!" Sally insisted.

She did, though.

Bad posture.

Flitting eye contact.

Mumbles a lot.

I used to be that way during freshman and sophomore years. I'd just dread having to go out in the hall to change classes. I felt like at any moment I could be bludgeoned for my sins of being too smart, not wearing expensive designer clothes, and hanging out with uncool people. I'd run in and out of the bathroom fast when the popular girls were in there.

Cedric used to skip school after getting hassled. Last year he decided he'd give it back in unusual ways. Now he'll walk up to a popular group, breathe like a degenerate, and hiss, "I'm a *bibliophile*." A bibliophile is a person who loves books, but not many people know that. He'll approach a group of cheerleaders and announce, "You know, girls, I'm *bipedal* . . ." That means he has two feet, but those cheerleaders scatter like squirrels. "I'm a *thespian*," he'll say lustfully. This means he's an actor, but you know how it is with some words. If they sound bad, people don't always wait around for the vocab lesson.

Jewel also has her own unique defense mechanism. When a carload of ICIs once drove alongside her car blaring loud music, she cranked up her tape of Gregorian chants to a deafening roar. Jewel said it put a new perspective on spirituality.

People were throwing jock-avoidance suggestions at Sally, but the advice wasn't sticking.

"I just want to ignore those people," she said sadly to the group.

"Can you do it, though?" I asked her.

She shrugged, mumbled, looked down.

See, for me, ignoring comes with its own set of problems. There are some people—Ed Looper is one of them—who can ignore the ICIs because he walks around in a cloud all day. If you want to get Looper's attention, it's best to trip him.

But *me*—sure, I can pretend I'm ignoring something or someone mean, but it doesn't help if deep down I'm steamed, and as I shove it farther and farther into the bottomless pit, the steam gets hotter.

So the biggest thing that's helped me cope is that I've stopped hoping that the mean in-crowders get punished for their cruelty. I think in some ways they have their punishments already. As my mom says, meanness never just goes out of a person—it goes back to them as well.

I look at the in-crowd table that's filling up. The beautiful Parker Cravens, Brent Fabrelli, the usual suspects. Doug Booker and Charlie Bass sit down too.

So what's inside you, Doug, that makes you so mean? If I were to put your heart under a microscope, what would I see?

Once Parker Cravens and I had to be lab partners. This was close to the worst news she'd gotten all year. She glared at me like I was a dead frog she had to dissect. Parker is stricken with *affluenza*, a condition that afflicts certain segments of the excruciatingly rich. She doesn't know or care how the other half lives; she thinks anyone who isn't wealthy is subterranean. At first I was ripped that she discounted me; then I started looking at her under the emotional microscope. I have X-ray vision from years of being ignored.

"Parker, do you like this class?" I asked.

She glanced at my nondesigner sports watch that I'd gotten for two bucks at a yard sale and shuddered. "My dad's making me take it. He's a doctor and he said I've got to know this dense stuff."

"What class would you rather be taking?"

She flicked a speck off her cashmere sweater and looked at me as if my question was totally insipid.

"No, really, Parker. Which one?"

"Art history," she said.

"Why don't you take it?"

Quiet voice. "My dad won't let me."

"Why not?"

"He wants me to be a doctor."

Parker would last two nanoseconds in med school.

"That's got to be hard," I offered.

"Like granite, Dana."

It's funny. No matter how mean she gets—and Parker can get mean—every time I see her now, I don't just think that she's the prettiest girl in school or the richest or the most popular; I think a little about how her father doesn't have a clue as to what she wants to be, and how much that must hurt.

My bedroom doesn't look like I feel. It's yellow and sunny. It's got posters of Albert Einstein and Eleanor Roosevelt and their best quotes.

Al's: *If at first the idea is not absurd, then there is no hope for it.*

Eleanor's: *No one can make you feel inferior without your consent.*

I flop on the bed wondering how come cruelty seems so easy for some people.

Wondering who decided how the boundary lines get drawn. You can never be too athletic, too popular, too gorgeous, or too rich, but you can be too smart and too nerdy.

My mom tells me that sometimes people try to control others when too many things are out of control in their own lives.

I walk to my closet and pull down the Ziploc bag in which I keep my old stuffed koala bear, Qantas. He can't handle life on the bed like my other animals—he's close to falling apart. Think Velveteen Rabbit. He was a big part of my childhood. I got him when I was four and kids started giving me a hard time in nursery school because I used words that were too big for them to understand. I've talked to him ever since.

I take Qantas out of the bag, look into his scratched plastic eyes.

This bear will not die.

I lost him at Disney World and found him. Lost him at the zoo and he turned up near the lion's cage. I always take him out when I've got a sticky problem. Maybe I'm remembering the power of childhood—the part that thinks a stuffed bear really holds the secrets to life.

And it's funny. As I hold him now, all kinds of things seem possible.

Like the Letter. I've been tossing the idea around all year: how I could write a letter to the ICIs, explain what life is like from my end of the lunchroom, and maybe things would get better at my school.

At first I thought it would be easy to write. It isn't. This is as far as I've gotten:

> To my classmates at the other end of the lunchroom:
>   This a difficult letter to write, but one that needs to be written.

Wrong, all wrong.

And there's the whole matter of how the letter will get distributed if I ever write it.

I could send it to the school paper.

Tack it to the front door with nails.

Print it up on T-shirts.

I think about the mangy comments that have been hurled at me this month.

Were you born or were you hatched?

Do you have to be my lab partner?

Do you have to have your locker next to mine?

I hug my bear. Some people go on-line with their problems. I go marsupial.

"Qantas, if I had the guts to write a letter to the in crowd at my school, this is what I'd like to say:

"This letter could be from the nerd with the thick glasses in computer lab. It could be from the 'zit girl' who won't look people in the eye because she's embarrassed about her skin. It could be from the guy with the nose ring who you call queer, or any of the kids whose sizes don't balance with your ideal.

"You know, I've got things inside me—dreams and nightmares, plans and mess-ups. In that regard, we have things in common. But we never seem to connect through those common experiences because I'm so different from you.

"My being different doesn't mean that you're better than me. I think you've always assumed that I want to be like you. But I want you to know something about kids like me. We don't want to. We just want the freedom to walk down the hall without seeing your smirks, your contempt, and your looks of disgust.

"Sometimes I stand far away from you in the hall and watch what you do to other people. I wonder why you've chosen to make the world a worse place.

"I wonder, too, what really drives the whole thing. Is it hate? Is it power? Are you afraid if you get too close to me and my friends that some of our uncoolness might rub off on you? I think what could really happen is that learning tolerance could make us happier, freer people.

"What's it going to be like when we all get older? Will we be more tolerant, or less because we haven't practiced it much? I think of the butterflies in the science museum. There are hundreds of them in cases. Hundreds of different kinds. If they were all the same, it would be so boring. You can't look at the blue ones or the striped ones and say they shouldn't have been born. It seems like nature is trying to tell us something. Some trees are tall, some are short. Some places have mountains, others have deserts. Some cities are always warm, some have different seasons. Flowers are different. Animals. Why do human beings think they have the right to pick who's best—who's acceptable and who's not?

"I used to give you control over my emotions. I figured that if you said I was gross and weird, it must be true. How you choose to respond to people is up to you, but I won't let you be my judge and jury. I'm going to remind you every chance I get that I have as much right to be on this earth as you."

I look at Qantas, remember bringing him to a teddy bear birthday party and being told he wasn't a real bear. I laugh about it now. He and I have never been mainstream.

I turn on my computer and begin to put it all down finally. The words just pour out, but I know the letter isn't for the ICIs and full-scale distribution.

It's for me.

And one other person.

I open my desk drawer where I keep my stash of emergency birthday cards. I pick one that reads: *It's your birthday. If you'd reminded me sooner, this card wouldn't be late.*

I sign the card; print the letter out, fold it in fourths so it will fit inside, and write Sally's name on the envelope.

Joan Bauer

The roots of "A Letter from the Fringe" go back to Joan Bauer's high school experiences as an overweight, unpopular girl who was picked on by the "in crowd." "I spent most of my adolescence feeling unworthy, rejected, and angry," she confesses. "I've always wondered what made mean people tick; always wondered if there was a key to unlock more of their humanity; and now I wonder what my life would have been like if I had been more like Dana."

In her early twenties Joan Bauer was a successful advertising and marketing salesperson, having inherited her talent from her father, "a salesman whom no one could say no to." Professional writing for magazines and newspapers followed, then screenwriting, which was cut short by a serious car accident. She then tried writing a novel about a high school girl who was determined to grow the biggest pumpkin in the state, titling it *Squashed*. When it won the Delacorte Prize for a first young adult novel and was subsequently named a Best Book for Young Adults by the American Library Association, a *School Library Journal* Best Book, as well as a Junior Library Guild selection, her writing career was launched.

Since then she has published a novel about a fifth-grade boy, called *Sticks*, and four novels for teens: *Thwonk, Rules of the Road, Backwater,* and *Hope Was Here.*

Those novels have won numerous awards, including an *American Bookseller* Pick of the Lists, ALA Best Books for Young Adults, and an ALA Quick Pick for Reluctant Readers. *Rules of the Road* has been especially honored, receiving the *Los Angeles Times* Book Prize for Young Adult Fiction and the Golden Kite Award.

Although her novels all deal with serious issues of identity and individualism, they are filled with humor, a quality Bauer inherited from her schoolteacher mother and her maternal grandmother, who was a famous storyteller.

Joan Bauer lives in Connecticut with her husband and teenage daughter. You can learn more about her on her website: www.joanbauer.com.

Guns for Geeks

Chris Crutcher

Sam's classmates have conflicting opinions about the relation-ship between guns and violence in America. Then Gene Taylor provides them with a perspective they will never forget.

I WONDER IF Mr. Dickerson would have beat out our National Anthem on Gene Taylor's butt at our second-grade Christmas party if he'd known how Gene would turn out. We were taking turns, hand-clapping the beat to our favorite songs, making the rest of the class guess, while we waited for our parents to bring cookies and punch and popcorn balls for our school Christmas party. For some reason Dickerson told Gene he was sorry Gene hadn't seen fit to wear red and green for the party like the rest of us. What a dipstick. You needed the obser-vation skills of Stevie Wonder to know Gene had but one pair of jeans and one shirt, a dingy little rag so old the blue cowboys were nearly indistinguishable from the gray background, the short sleeves hemmed so many times they would barely hold thread.

Gene was a stick of a thing who needed the extra two pounds of dirt he wore like underwear to make the bottom five percent of the growth chart. He was usually as quiet as he was poor, but this time he called Dickerson by his last name minus the last five letters. He didn't say it very loud but Dickerson heard him, and though the man's expression didn't change, the vein in his temple popped up like a garden hose and he called Gene to him. Gene didn't move and Dickerson said he'd better. Gene said, "You can't make me," and Dickerson got up and did.

"See if you can get this one, kids," he said, forcing Gene over his knee, and he began to spank out a tune. Gene kicked at him, but Dickerson had him pinned. Most of us laughed at first; few had any idea what it was to be Gene Taylor.

Gene was mad now, embarrassed past caring, and he said Dickerson better let him up, and Dickerson said, "Oh, had I?" and paddled harder. Gene tried harder to kick him but Dickerson forced his legs down with his elbow and coolly played his butt like a timpani. "Double time," he told us.

"Why don't you go home and spank your fat wife?" Gene growled between clenched teeth, and his buttocks were suddenly a bass drum. Nobody thought it was funny anymore and we started making wild guesses, feeling the heat of Gene's predicament, imagining our own seven-year-old butts in the same place.

"She's so fat, I bet she can't even do the nasty thing," Gene hollered, and Dickerson's hands became mallets.

"Bet if you tried this on her, your hand would disappear," Gene screamed. None of us had ever heard this many words from him.

"'The Star-Spangled Banner'!" I yelled. "It's 'The Star-Spangled Banner'!"

"Which verse?" Dickerson yelled back, now beating Gene's butt so hard it jarred his teeth.

That incident is just a blip on the screen of Gene Taylor's life. I doubt he even remembers it. My mother is a child therapist and my dad works for the Department of Children's Services, and we've been a receiving home for kids being put into foster care as long as I can remember. Gene was at our house probably ten times, sometimes so hungry he couldn't keep from stuffing himself like a famine victim at the dinner table, and sometimes sporting some really creative bruises and burns. Recently he lived with only his mother, her latest boyfriend having taken off with Gene's older sister. And that's just what I know. Imagine what the whole truth might be.

Our town of about fifteen thousand lies in the heart of West Central Washington hunting country, near one of the state's largest lakes, only thirty miles from the Canadian border. In this neck of the woods, if a guy were offered the choice between a gun rack and a spare tire as an option on a brand-new pickup, he'd say, "What the hell do I need with a spare tire?" Last summer when my brother, T.J., returned from a trip to San Francisco with a bumper sticker reading I SUPPORT THE RIGHT TO ARM BEARS, he didn't just lose the sticker, he lost the bumper.

T.J. and I would be twins if you went by our birthdays, but my parents were smart enough to get him from a deeper, wider, adoptive gene pool. If I didn't know better, I'd suspect his parents were Michael Jordan and Babe Didrikson; and if I didn't know better I'd think mine were Peewee Herman and Ally McBeal. It's not really that bad, but it is safe to say T.J. comes by his marvelous athletic skills naturally, and I have to work like a coal miner in the Arctic for mine.

I don't get it about guns. They have one purpose and that's to put holes in things, and after what we've been through, I have a feeling the framers of the Constitution would think twice before "framing" the Second Amendment. My first lesson about guns came in what I thought, before last week, was the hard way. Montgomery Cambridge, a kid in my class in junior high school, was a target shooter; still is. That's a handle that brings your share of crapola if you happen to be just under five feet tall (he's only five five today) and maybe eighty pounds carrying a couple rolls of nickels in your pockets. And horn-rimmed glasses, for crying out loud. The guy's parents own two Eye-Spy franchise stores in Spokane where they specialize in eyewear for the fashion-conscious, and Monty spends three hours perusing the inventory to pick a pair of black horn-rims.

At any rate, for a fleeting moment I was fascinated with the idea of blowing away forest animals to help you bond with your dad (even though that's the last way my dad would bond with me). So when Monty asked if I wanted to go pop a few tin cans, I was willing to let him consider himself my new friend long enough to log some shootin' time. We filled a couple of garbage bags with tin cans and bottles from around the neighborhood and dragged them into the wilds behind his house. I didn't—and don't—know much about guns, but when he brought that pistol out of its cushioned case and laid it in my palm, I knew—in the way you know when you touch a Stradivarius violin or sit in a Jaguar—that I was handling a classy instrument. We spent a couple hours picking off the cans and bottles—his five to my one—and after my last turn, a tree squirrel scampered through the pine needles in front of us and started up the skinny trunk of a lodgepole pine about twenty feet away. I drew a bead on him just to see what it felt like. He scurried to a low branch, hopped out toward the end, then stopped and looked at me.

Somebody should tell all wild animals caught in the crosshairs of a fine shooting instrument, don't stop. Still, I wasn't going to shoot him; I really wasn't. I held him in the sight. Remember, I hadn't hit but one target all afternoon and Monty had been delighting in kicking my ass at the only thing in the world he could possibly kick anybody's ass at. But suddenly it was as if the squirrel and I had an agreement. A lesson would be learned here. I would shoot him, and he would be shot. With both eyes open like Monty had taught me, I squeezed the trigger slowly, and pop! The squirrel dropped to the ground like a rock. He didn't struggle in the leaves or try to get up and run or even blink. He lay stone dead.

Monty shrieked in horrified astonishment, jerking the pistol out of my hands, screaming, "What are you doing? What are you doing? Oh, God! Look what you did!" But the excitement of the kill filled my chest, and I told him to get a grip, it was only a squirrel, and ran to retrieve my trophy. Only no trophy awaited me—just a dead animal, eyes open, looking at me, past me, through me, telling me I had broken a sacred trust, and I understood it in a wave that rolled through my chest and into my throat. I don't know how long I crouched, looking at him, running my finger over his soft tan back and side, wishing I could step back over that moment when the light pressure of my finger on the trigger had brought the hammer down. When I looked toward the fence, Monty was nowhere to be seen and I was alone in the warm fall afternoon with the breeze caressing the branches of the trees high above me, and a life I had taken for no reason other than to see if I could. I scooped away some dirt to make a shallow grave, placed the squirrel's warm body in, and covered him over. I didn't ask forgiveness. I couldn't have looked at it this way then, but if good came out of that afternoon it is that I have never drawn a bead on another living thing.

I don't tell that story often. In fact, I've never told it before. It's kind of a sappy tale the Disney people would reject on sight as too corny. Besides, no reason to place a "Wussy" label on yourself more times than your life places it there naturally. But I never forget it or the feeling that goes with it. Like I said, I don't get it about guns. I have to agree with my mom that nature doesn't need the kinds of surprises they create.

Don't get me wrong. I'm not a pacifist. I could kill if threatened, or I could hunt for survival; but not for fun. It's no damn fun.

That's the secret history I took into Mr. Beemer's U.S. Government class discussion about what might have been in the forefathers' minds when they wrote the Bill of Rights. Regarding freedom of expression we agreed only that it's pushing it to yell "Fire!" at a crowded indoor rock concert, and were ironically attempting a better understanding of our right to bear arms.

Beemer is boys' basketball coach and an athlete on my brother's level, but academics is even more important to him than athletics. He's one of those teachers with lots of opinions, and he's quick to tell you exactly what they are up front so they don't get in the way of his teaching. He's right there to challenge your every thought, but always gives your ideas respect. You can pretty much figure he's "liberal" when it comes to politics, and even more liberal in his teaching style; like one day Janelle Arnold said in class that a book she'd read should be burned. So Beemer took us all down to the library, found the book, paid the librarian for it, and marched us to the football field, where we promptly burned it. He said, "There. Done. How does that feel?"

Janelle said, "No, I meant we should burn all of them," to which Beemer said that would be a completely differ-ent matter, and we had a great, screaming discussion about censorship right there on the football field.

On this day, amidst our Second Amendment discus-sion, Beemer was promoting the idea of context. "How many of you—and I'd like a show of hands here rather than pistols—believe the framers of our Constitution considered when they included that particular right that we might someday have guns that fired more than one bullet with one squeeze of the trigger?"

His question met blank stares.

"Or that our society might turn out to be one of the world's most violent in the new millennium."

More stares.

"That would be the year 2000."

We knew what the millennium was. "What's the point?" Rob Garner asked.

"That had they known the mayhem that would be created with the arms everyone was bearing, they might have put some qualifiers in."

"Guns don't kill people," Roy Salley said, speaking of bumper stickers.

"I know," Beemer said back, "people kill people. But they do it with guns."

"Not always," Rob said. "An old guy in Spokane was beaten to death with a golf club last week. How come people don't ask for a ban on golf clubs?"

"Actually, my wife asked for that just last week," Beemer said. I think Rob has been doing his homework in the kitchen one time too many, while his dad and his dad's buddies hold their weekly militia meeting around the ol' potbellied stove.

T.J. said, "When was the last time you heard of a drive-by golf clubbing, Rob?"

Beemer smiled and most of the class laughed. "Don't get me wrong, guys. I'm not trying to rewrite the Constitution, or remove your right to bear arms. I'm just asking—if the context had been different, would the framers have written it differently?" Actually, I think Beemer would rewrite that part of the Constitution if he could, but Rob's parents are in the office complaining about some teacher or curriculum often enough that they could save money hiring a lobbyist. No way he wanted to get caught in their philosophical crosshairs without a lot more at stake. And if Roy Salley's dad thought the local social studies teacher was the kind of liberal douche-bag Commie who voiced his opposition to every man, woman, child, and unborn, having the right to at least as many automatic weapons as he or she has fingers, why, he'd just have to march down to the school and call him out.

Rob said, "It's all relative. The good guys and the bad guys have access to the same sophisticated firearms." One thing about Garner, he can talk.

Monty Cambridge, with whom I have regained a little credibility as a human over the years, said he thinks firearms should only be used in regulated competitions. He started to tell the story of a friend of his who'd once gunned down a tree squirrel in cold blood, but Roy interrupted him.

"That thing you shoot isn't even classified as a weapon," Roy said to Monty. "Actually, Coach is right, some people shouldn't have access to guns. Guys like you and Taylor should be limited to water pistols and Red Ryder BB guns. Think I'm gonna have a T-shirt made: No Guns for Geeks." Gene Taylor's seat was empty; he hadn't been in school for a couple of days. Roy never passes up a chance to goad him, though, even in his absence.

Beemer's eyes narrowed. "Looks like we've retreated to our 'freedom of expression' discussion, Roy. Tell you what, you feel free to keep on expressing yourself that way, and I'll feel free to express myself at grade time."

Linda Cross raised her hand, and I flinched. Linda's little brother had killed her littler brother last year playing with their father's handgun, there for purposes of protection and supposedly out of reach. She said,

"Maybe people kill people, but if Christopher hadn't gotten his hands on that gun, Marvin wouldn't be dead." She glared at Rob, then at Roy. "Even if he could have gotten his hands on a golf club."

It was a little off the point, but even those two didn't want to take it on.

I looked out the window then to avoid the discomfort I felt about Linda's remark, and what must be an awful emptiness about her brothers. I mean, it's hard to know whether I'd rather be the kid that's dead or the kid that did it.

I saw a dark figure moving across the lawn then. Now I'm aware of a disturbing sense of something truly sinister, but at the time it was no more than an unsettled inkling. I'm also aware now what an amazing coincidence it was that we were having that class discussion at that particular moment.

Beemer called it to a halt, partly because the bell was about to ring, and partly, I think, because for a philosophical discourse, this was getting rugged.

The door opened, and we looked up to see Gene Taylor in a long rider's coat, leather cowboy hat and boots, his face contorted into a grim intention that certainly changed our lives forever.

Let me clear something up. No matter how many times you see somebody whacked in the movies or on TV, it doesn't desensitize you even a little bit to the real thing. Gene stands in the doorway like some dark avenger. In that first moment he looks ridiculous—cartoonish—then the front of the coat swings back and, scanning the room with narrow eyes, he brings up a lever-action .30-.30.

He shoots Roy Salley first, in the head. Roy is there, a recognition on his face, staring down the barrel, then gone. It unfolds in slow motion. Roy pitches backward, his head striking the blackboard like a melon—then there is only vacancy.

Megan Gratten is next, probably only because she sits next to Roy there in the back of the room. Her eyes widen in astonishment as the bullet rips through her neck, then she lies tipped over, an awful sucking sound coming from the wound. Low moans escape terrified throats. I am so aware of weight, of gravity's imposing force, welding me to my spot. Something inside me says do something. It is Gene Taylor, whose butt doubled for Dickerson's bass drum, whom I have watched come and go from our foster house like a church mouse; a wall-hugger who makes a career of being invisible, now reducing the toughest of us to our knees. His eyes are dark and consumed as he swings the rifle barrel in search of his next victim.

Gene tells us to put our heads on our desks. When no one responds he screams it, firing two more rounds. One strikes Mr. Beemer in the shoulder and the other slams into Carly Pruitt's stomach. Carly is my girlfriend and best friend. She looks at the wound, back at Gene, and simply says, "Gene," before crumpling to the floor. I leap from my chair then, kneel and cradle her head in my lap, only to look up at the long tunnel that is his rifle. Carly breathes shallow gulps of air, her eyes shut tight against the pain. I say, "Don't, man. Please."

Our eyes meet and his finger twitches on the trigger, and maybe he remembers I was decent to him in our home, because he motions with the barrel for everyone to put their heads down. They do so in unison. Stifled sobs leak out all over the room. I don't move, only hold Carly's head tight against my chest. Mr. Beemer is conscious, slumped forward at his desk gripping his shoulder, groaning, blood trickling down his forearm onto the back of his hand, then dripping to the floor as if from a leaky faucet. I hope his mind is working; Gene isn't finished.

"You too," Gene says, swinging the barrel back toward me, motioning me to my desk. I start to lay Carly's head onto the floor, but she whimpers, "Sam, don't leave." God, she sounds in such pain.

"I can't," I say to Gene, bringing her head back to my chest. "I can't leave her, man."

He glares at me then, his lip curls, and I listen for the bang. "Keep your heads down!" he screams at the rest of the class, eyes locked mine for that dreadful moment, and swings the barrel away, leaving his back to me. I beg myself to rise; can't.

They bury their eyes, closing out the sight of the bodies on the floor and Mr. Beemer gasping at his desk. The one person not terrorized is my brother, T.J. He drops his head like the rest, but I catch his eye peeking past the crook of his elbow. We stare at each other a moment, then he fixes on Gene.

"Things are going to change around here," Gene says, a forcefulness in his voice I've never heard. "The first will be last and the last will be first." He chuckles. "The first will be dead and the last will be first." He points the rifle at Johnny Waller now, a quick, first-string point guard—with a quicker mouth—and a straight-A student. He walks toward him, his back still to me, then glances over his shoulder to smile at me, and shoots him through the back of the head point-blank. Johnny slumps like a sack of potatoes. The report of the rifle brings a collective moan.

"Get it together," Gene says to Johnny's still corpse. "Get it together." *Get it together* is Johnny's rallying cry bringing the ball up court—it's also what he said to Gene Taylor in front of our sophomore speech class when Gene froze in the face of a one-minute improvisational speech two years ago.

A lone cry escapes somewhere in the back of the room. Monty Cambridge. "Shut up!" Gene screams, and the sobbing ceases. "No crybabies. Crybabies and whiners are next." Monty's head pops up and I catch his terrified look, before he forces his head back down through the sheer power of psychic will. Somehow Gene doesn't see. "Big mouths first, crybabies and whiners next," he repeats.

"Stop him," Carly whispers in my ear. "Sam, you have to."

What can I do? I say it with my eyes, paralyzed as the rest.

Gene stands, his back still to me, looking monstrous as the executioner. I have a chance at him, I think, if I can just steal a little closer. Gently, quietly, I place Carly's head on the floor, but my legs are like concrete. All I can see, all I can imagine, is Gene turning and killing me. Again, T.J.'s eye catches mine.

At the desk Beemer pulls himself up, stands wobbly legged, holding his shoulder, taking slow, deep breaths. He moves around the desk.

"Let's see, who's next?" Gene says, looking over the students bent over their desks. "Who else called me pussy?"

Beemer stands up straight. "Gene," he says, and Gene turns, startled. "You have to stop."

"Stop?" Gene laughs, his voice shrill. "I'm just getting started. All these scores to settle, so little time." He looks Beemer up and down. "You're not looking so good, sir. Why don't you have a seat?"

He turns back to the students. "Now, where were we?" His eyes fall on Albert Jewell. He removes a pistol from his belt, walks toward him. Albert is a buddy of Roy's and I see him twitch as Gene's boots click toward him on the hardwood floor, perhaps remembering some specific time when he called Gene a pussy. I truly believe I am looking at a dead man. Carly lies motionless now, and still I am frozen.

Gene raises the pistol toward Albert's head.

"Pussy." Beemer says it from behind. "If you're looking for people who called you pussy, I'm your guy."

"Never heard you say that, sir," Gene says without turning around. "I shot you because you didn't stop them."

"In the teacher's lounge," Beemer says. "I called you that in the teacher's lounge all the time. 'Wouldn't have Taylor on any of my teams. Way too big a pussy.'"

Sweat pours off Beemer's brow and his knees buckle, but he catches himself. Then through gritted teeth, "You slimy little pussy, Taylor."

Gene turns, eyes blazing, jaw set. He walks toward Beemer, positions himself to see the class as well. Still only I am in his visual twilight zone. Beemer's eyes plead to me.

Gene says, "Get on your knees, sir."

Their eyes lock a moment, and Beemer slowly kneels, his shirtsleeve soaked in blood. He closes his eyes.

"Open your mouth," Gene says. He laughs. "I want to see you explode."

A long hesitation. Beemer says, "No."

"Open it!"

"I can't, Gene. If you're going to shoot me, just do it."

"Put the barrel of the gun in your mouth and I'll let one person go," Gene says.

Beemer glances around at the class, his eyes lock on me, then T.J. It's the alley-oop look from open gym night; Beemer signaling T.J. to go for the slam dunk. He starts to open his mouth, then, "No, it has to be more than one."

Gene appears frustrated for the first time, unsure. He hesitates. "How many?"

"All of them."

"Get real."

"All of them, Gene, or you don't get to watch my head explode."

"Open your goddamn mouth!" he screams, and his voice jars me loose. I leap up as he turns; I never had a chance. But from his knees, Beemer blocks him like an offensive guard, knocking him off balance as T.J. springs headlong from his desk, snatching the gun as Gene pulls the trigger, burying the bullet in the ceiling. Beemer pins Gene to the floor as a student pulls the classroom door open and teachers swarm in. In the distance, sirens wail.

We probably could have predicted what would happen next by watching old CNN footage. Reporters swarmed the place, beginning with the local TV station, followed by the networks. Even after Columbine, which changed the portrait of school violence forever, this one captured the media's attention because of Gene's plan. It was his intention, one by one and in cold blood, to kill us all. He told the police that.

My brother and I dodged the media. He simply didn't want to have anything to do with them and got in his car and drove. Our parents were out of town, so it would be late in the night before they got back. I probably could have switched on the "hero" mode, except for one thing: I didn't feel like a hero.

I got away from school out the back way before the local news media could catch me, and hightailed it to the hospital to see how Carly and Mr. Beemer were. Nobody would tell me anything about Carly, other than that she was alive and in surgery, but Beemer had given explicit instructions that if either T.J. or I showed up, he wanted to see us.

He was sitting up in his bed; his wife next to him in a chair when I peeked around the corner.

He said, "Sammy, come on in."

I walked over and he put his good hand on my forearm. "How you doing?"

"Okay, I guess. How about you?"

He looked at his arm. "Well, I've been shot."

He told me T.J. and I had saved a lot of lives, that he'd never have had a shot at Gene if I hadn't diverted his attention, and who knows who else might have been hit if T.J. hadn't gone for the gun.

I tried to hold it in, but it blurted out of me. "Yeah, but what about Johnny?"

"What do you mean?"

"Coach, Gene had his back to me. I couldn't have stopped him from shooting Roy or Megan or even Carly. But his back was to me before he killed Johnny." I fought for air. "I froze."

"Don't do that," Beemer said, and he said it like a coach. "You'll think of a thousand times you could have moved, and so will I and so will every other person in the room. We did what we did and that's it."

I stood gawking, almost sorry I'd said it, sorry I had let anyone know what I feared most. He motioned me closer, grabbed my forearm with his good hand. "Sam, listen to me. All of us in that room know something about ourselves that we didn't know before today. Nothing's ever going to be the same for anyone who was there. But there's only one person to blame for this, and that's Gene. He came into the room with his guns and opened fire. Everything that happened after that was in response to it. Okay?"

I took a deep breath, saw Gene's back again, saw Johnny slump forward.

"Sam, there's no one in the world I'd rather have had in your place today than you."

I tried to respond, but I choked on it, and Beemer pulled me closer and hugged me with that powerful arm. "Don't ever forget that," he said.

I wanted to believe what Coach said, and maybe as time goes on it'll be easier. But I can't shake the sensation of being paralyzed, of knowing some of my best friends, my girlfriend, my *brother*, for God's sake, stood to die, and I couldn't move.

A part of me wanted to go lie in the sweet embrace of my family. Another part wanted to find all the kids in the class to see if they'd seen what I'd seen. Still another part wanted to be alone until I could quiet the voices; think Johnny Waller's name without my heart clogging my throat.

No high school or junior high in the country hasn't had to imagine this in recent years. The West, the Midwest, the South, all have killing stories that have floated up to us. Every time you see someone on CNN after an incident like this, they say, We thought it could never happen here, or simply, Why? But I don't think it would have helped me one bit to know why. I just wanted it not to have happened.

The following days went by in a blur for me. There were candlelight vigils, calls for forgiveness, potluck dinners at churches; my flood of relief at hearing Carly would recover was juxtaposed with the knowledge that Johnny Waller and Megan Gratten and Roy Salley would never sing another song or dribble another ball or see another sunset. And funerals. I couldn't tell you which came first or what was said at any one—only that whatever was said, it wasn't enough. It wasn't right.

I jump up one morning, dog-tired and so early it's almost still the night before, and hop into my Geo Storm to drive through the deserted streets of Wolf River toward Waller's Chevron out on the two-lane that leads the forty miles to the East-West freeway. I don't know what I'm doing up this early; I barely caught three hours sleep. But something in me thinks if I make myself tired enough I'll get all that's happened under control in my head. That's what I want; almost more than I want Johnny and Megan and Roy back. I just want control.

I pull up next to the one self-serve pump. Mr. Waller's an older guy—Johnny wasn't born until he was in his late forties—and has always been quick to tell us how modern-day service stations have gone way to hell. In his day, by God, the attendant pumped the gas and checked the oil, water, and fan belts without asking, and washed every damn window in the car if you requested it and offered to check the air pressure in your tires, and why the hell did we think they called it a service station? And by the way, a service station was never meant to be no damn 7-Eleven. Needless to say, Waller's gets a lot of business from older people in town who remember things the same way he does.

Mr. Waller is inside counting bills and change into the cash register. I'm desperate to know if anyone has talked with him about that day—if anyone has told him Gene Taylor's back was to me for what seemed like an eternity before he shot Johnny, and that I didn't move.

I top off my tank and walk inside to pay. Mr. Waller says, "What brings you out this early?" His voice is flat, his eyes huge and watery, sad.

"Guess I've been getting too much sleep," I say. I look back out at the pump and hand him a ten. "Looks like you owe me a buck fifty."

He hands me a bill and two quarters. "How ya been?"

"Okay, I guess. You know."

He nods. God, does he have any idea? "Wanted to thank you again for Johnny's funeral, for carryin' the casket."

"That's okay," I say, realizing how dumb it sounds before I get it out of my mouth. I watch his thick fingers as he closes the cash register; one of those ancient ones with a crank on the side in case the power fails. Those thick, strong hands I noticed at the funeral.

"That's a hard thing to do," he says. "Carry a dead classmate."

I say, "There have been a lot of hard things around here lately." I have such an urge to scream at him how sorry I am that I didn't move. I'm feeling like all those little kids who have passed through our house; I want something in my life to be congruent.

"An' more to come, more'n likely," he says. "I want you to answer me a question," he says then. "Truthfully."

My heart leaps into my throat, clogs it. I take a quick breath. "Sure."

"You think my boy was a smartass?"

"Naw—" I say it too fast.

"I asked for the truth."

"Yeah, well, maybe. No more than me. No more than a lot of guys."

"He liked you."

I don't know what to say. Johnny and I played on the same teams and I used to hang out here at the gas station sometimes, but usually with three or four other guys. I wouldn't have counted him among my best friends.

"You think his big mouth got him shot?"

I flash to that day in sophomore speech class when he told Gene Taylor to "get it together," watched Gene turn red and drop his gaze to the floor, then sit down without a word. Johnny shook his head and said, "Jesus, Taylor."

Mr. Waller's call for the truth rings in my head. I say, "Yeah, maybe. Johnny wasn't exactly, like, sensitive, but hey, who is?"

Mr. Waller hoists himself up onto the counter next to the cash register, takes the grease rag out of his back pocket, and wipes his big hands slowly. "I'm afraid I might a taught him to be that way," he says. "I'm kinda the quiet type, always felt a bit afraid to push things." It's almost as if he's talking to someone else, or no one, staring at that spot a few inches from his nose. "Wanted him to stand up, not be like me."

"Hey," I tell him, "there are lots of guys around with bigger mouths than Johnny. I mean, who knows why Gene picked who he picked?"

"Well, he picked the Salley boy for one," Mr. Waller says. "That tells me a lot." He's quiet a few seconds. "I'd just feel more peaceful if I thought my boy wasn't gone 'cause of somethin' I done."

I remember Beemer's words. "Johnny's gone because Gene Taylor was fucked up," I say. "Pardon my language."

Mr. Waller considers for another few seconds. "It's a minefield," he says. "This life."

Mr. Waller was a foot soldier in the Korean War. He knows what a minefield is. Suddenly I just want to help him; to say some truth that takes the edge off. I decide on the big one. "Before he shot Johnny," I say hesitantly, "Gene was . . . Well, he turned his back to me."

Mr. Waller's head comes up. He watches me, doesn't speak. The seconds are days.

"I mean, I don't know if anyone told you—" I can't read his face; he seems to be drinking me in, and the silence is killing me. "I don't know whether—" I feel choked, panicky. "Maybe if I'd moved faster—"

He's looking deep into me now, into my soul, won't tell me what he sees—the depth of his contempt.

"I was scared," I say, and move toward the door. "I was so damn scared. I'm sorry, Mr. Waller."

In my peripheral vision I see him moving toward the door as I climb into my car, think he's going to yell something at me, but I want to disappear so I keep my eyes focused straight ahead and pull out, catching a glimpse of him in my rear-view mirror standing out on the concrete, his hand half raised.

There are still a couple of hours before school starts, and dawn is crisp and cold now, thin sheets of frost everywhere. I don't know exactly where I'm driving but I need to get my thoughts under control, and soon I find the road getting narrower and narrower, turning from pavement to dirt as I wind my way up into the area where the loggers used to reign—past the old Carter place where I shot the squirrel with Monty Cambridge's .22 target pistol. The road winds ahead through a number of switchbacks as it climbs, and I hold down on the throttle as far as I dare, the neglected washboard road rattling my teeth.

There has to be some way to make sense of all this, to stop the unraveling. What can I say to Mr. Waller now? How can I get him to understand the feeling of lead in my legs as I watch in what now seems like slow motion, as Gene Taylor moves across the room, smiles as he looks back over his shoulder at me, then puts the gun to the back of Johnny Waller's head and pulls the trigger. The report of the pistol is muffled, the barrel is so close to Johnny's hair. I see it, the window of opportunity, but as I think it, it closes, with a bang. Everybody—T.J., Beemer, Mom and Dad—tells me it would have been foolish to move then, but Johnny Waller is dead and his father might still be standing out there on the frosty concrete at his service station, waving me back to tell him why his son is gone.

At a broad clearing near the top of the mountain, I pull off, shutting down the engine but feeling my body continue to vibrate to its ghostly memory of the washboard road. Above me the sky turns a pale pink. I roll down my window, let the cold air rush in as I take a deep breath, trying to fill my body with something clean.

For a long while I sit, thoughts shooting through my head in a random storm. I pull my coat tight around me, lay the seat back a bit, and stare at the last bright star. The thoughts pass in single file, in twos, in stampedes. I don't light on one, but release to feel them rush through—images actually, more than words: Gene standing in the doorway to the classroom. Gene leaning over a plate of food in our house, embarrassingly ravenous. Roy Salley's smug look as he taps Gene on one shoulder and slaps the opposite side of his head as Gene turns to look. Johnny Waller with his head on his desk. The back of Gene's head as he walks away. The look in T.J.'s eye. Beemer in his hospital bed. Carly bleeding on the floor. Mr. Waller's sad face.

It turns out Mr. Waller only wanted to wave me back to say he didn't blame me, that he couldn't stand it if I blamed myself. The newspeople kept trying to make T.J. and Beemer and me into heroes, and Beemer finally convinced me they needed to do that for reasons that had nothing to do with any of us. In a short time they were gone.

The talk now is all about forgiveness. What I'm pretty sure of is that no one knows what that is. Local ministers were calling for it the day of the shootings. How can you forgive someone who has done something you can't even wrap your mind around. And if you're Gene Taylor, what does it feel like to be forgiven? Would you even know? Would it matter? Because along with the talk of forgiveness, sometimes in the same sentence, is talk of who is to blame. It's as if we can't get past any of this unless we find out who to hang it on.

Well, I've had some time to think, and I have a theory. No one is to blame. Everyone is to blame. I mean, Gene is to blame because he did it; no one can argue with that. But when I remember his face—his eyes—it's hard to think he had any control over what he was doing. We could blame his parents—a mother for being there too much and a dad for not being there at all—but it's not as if they sat around and said "Let's fuck up our kid so bad that he goes out and opens fire." It's not hard to imagine that *their* folks did a worse than mediocre job of parenting too. I think the business of assessing blame is just a snake eating its own tail.

Mr. Waller made the statement I like best. He said, "I don't care who's to blame. My son is dead and that's never going to be any different." Don't get me wrong. I hate Gene Taylor for what he did. And I hate him because of how cowardly I felt, and still feel, for what *I* did and didn't do when I had to face him. But I also can't help seeing him at my house, gorging himself, satiating one hunger while not touching the other; hiding his scars, grateful for the respite and at the same time resentful toward me, because he has never had the things I take for granted—food, love, Nikes, a girlfriend. Gene Taylor had to feel embarrassed coming to our house. How messed up is that? A guy gets treated like shit, then has to be ashamed when folks discover that he's a guy people treat like shit.

I go out to Waller's Chevron every Thursday morning at the crack of dawn. Mr. Waller and I have breakfast and miss Johnny together. When I got there this morning, he had already broken out the donuts and coffee, and was sitting with his feet up on the front desk, reading the paper. The headline said, "Taylor Decision Due Today." Mr Waller looked up and said hi, then went back to the article. "Says here if they try him as a juvenile, he's out on his twenty-first birthday at the latest. If they try him as an adult he could get life with no possibility of parole." He put the paper down and smiled that tired smile. "They're trying to figure out how to punish him," he said, slowly shaking his head. "Hell, don't they know guys like Gene Taylor are punished *before* they do their deed?"

Now, what are we going to do about that?

Chris Crutcher

Having spent a career as a child and family therapist focusing on abuse and domestic violence, Chris Crutcher is all too familiar with wounded kids like Gene Taylor in "Guns for Geeks." Although the story is fiction, it has its basis in the horrifying realities that have occurred in our nation's schools recently and provides a fitting climax to this book.

For his outstanding literary achievements, Chris Crutcher received the Margaret A. Edwards Award from the American Library Association in 2000. In addition, he has received the National Intellectual Freedom Award from the National Council of Teachers of English and SLATE (Support for the Learning and Teaching of English) as well as the ALAN Award from the Assembly on Literature for Adolescents of the NCTE.

Crutcher is the author of six highly regarded novels—*Running Loose, Stotan!, The Crazy Horse Electric Game, Chinese Handcuffs, Staying Fat for Sarah Byrnes,* and *Ironman*—and a book of short stories called *Athletic Shorts.* Every one of those books has been selected as an ALA Best Book for Young Adults, and two of them—*Stotan!* and *Athletic Shorts*—are listed among the 100 Best of the Best Books for Young Adults published between 1967 and 1992. He has also written the screenplays for *Staying Fat for Sarah Byrnes, Running Loose,* and *The Crazy*

Horse Electric Game, though none of them has yet been filmed.

His newest novel, *Whale Talk,* is about a high school swim team with very little ability and no swimming pool who find dignity in their sport and bring new meaning to loyalty in tough situations.

Resources

BOOKS

Cobain, Bev. *When Nothing Matters Anymore: A Survival Guide for Depressed Teens*. Minneapolis: Free Spirit, 1998.

Columbia University's Health Education Program. *The "Go Ask Alice" Book of Answers: A Guide to Good Physical, Sexual, and Emotional Health*. New York: Henry Holt, 1998.

Desetta, A., and Sybil Wolin, eds. *The Struggle to Be Strong: True Stories by Teens About Overcoming Tough Times*. Minneapolis: Free Spirit, 2000.

HELP LINES

National Crisis Line: 1-800-785-8111

Covenant House, a safe place for teens: 1-800-999-9999

WEBSITES

www.thehelplineusa.com—24-hour counseling on a variety of problems, including depression, suicide, drug and alcohol dependence, and other stresses and crises.

www.suicidehotlines.com—A suicide prevention website with an extensive list of crisis-counseling phone numbers.

www.teenadviceonline.org—Support and advice on teen-specific concerns.

www.labs.net/dixonm/raven.html—Raven D   te dedicated to helping persecuted kids cope.

www.outproud.org/menu.html—The wel the National Coalition for Gay, Lesbia gender Youth.

www.shashdot.org—A Web 'zine "Voices From The Hellmouth" by teen comments in this book's int

www.teenadviceonline.org—Support and advice on teen-specific concerns.

www.labs.net/dixonm/raven.html—Raven Days, a website dedicated to helping persecuted kids cope.

www.outproud.org/menu.html—The website of !OutProud!, the National Coalition for Gay, Lesbian, Bisexual & Transgender Youth.

www.shashdot.org—A Web 'zine that includes the article "Voices From The Hellmouth" by Jon Katz, from which the teen comments in this book's introduction were quoted.

Resources

BOOKS

Cobain, Bev. *When Nothing Matters Anymore: A Survival Guide for Depressed Teens*. Minneapolis: Free Spirit, 1998.

Columbia University's Health Education Program. *The "Go Ask Alice" Book of Answers: A Guide to Good Physical, Sexual, and Emotional Health*. New York: Henry Holt, 1998.

Desetta, A., and Sybil Wolin, eds. *The Struggle to Be Strong: True Stories by Teens About Overcoming Tough Times*. Minneapolis: Free Spirit, 2000.

HELP LINES

National Crisis Line: 1-800-785-8111

Covenant House, a safe place for teens: 1-800-999-9999

WEBSITES

www.thehelplineusa.com—24-hour counseling on a variety of problems, including depression, suicide, drug and alcohol dependence, and other stresses and crises.

www.suicidehotlines.com—A suicide prevention website with an extensive list of crisis-counseling phone numbers.